The Trumpiad

THE

❧TRUMPIAD❧

BOOK the FIRST

Being a Satirical Work in Twelve Cantos on the Turbulent First Year of the Administration of the Forty-Fifth President of the United States of America

And the Sundry Calamities that Befell the Nation during the Annus Horribilis, Two Thousand and Seventeen of the Common Era

By that Veritable Vesuvius of Verse

Mr. Martin Rowe

who, formerly being a subject of Her Majesty, Elizabeth the Second, by the Grace of God, of Great Britain, Queen, Defender of the Faith, and having entirely renounced and abjured all allegiance and fidelity to any foreign prince, potentate, state, or sovereignty, and now a proud citizen of these United States currently residing in Kings County, New York, has thusly exploded in this molten outpouring for the purpose of rousing his fellow Americans from their slumbers—or, if not that, then providing them with ashes in which they might sit.

To the American People
(May God Save Us)

&

Evander Lomke
colleague, comrade, conversationalist, collaborator,
collector of coincidences, quoter, quipster, and quirky antiquarian

Contents

Author's Note ix

Canto I: January...1
Canto II: February..13
Canto III: March...23
Canto IV: April...35
Canto V: May..47
Canto VI: June..61
Canto VII: July...73
Canto VIII: August...85
Canto IX: September......................................97
Canto X: October..109
Canto XI: November.....................................121
Canto XII: December....................................133

Dramatis Personae 145
Greco-Roman Mythological Characters and Places 153
Other Literary Characters 155
Acknowledgments 157
About the Author

Author's Note

WHEN HISTORY BOOKS are written about 2017 and the year that preceded it (assuming that something called "writing" survives, such things as "books" remain, and any human settlements exist to recollect anything in the way of "history"), it may be possible to consider with a degree of equanimity the character of the forty-fifth president of the United States, the reasons for his election in November 2016, and what either tell us about the people who voted for him or those who thought it unimportant to vote at all.

Will his occupation of the White House be viewed as an aberration, an interregnum, the signifier of the sorry end of a certain manifestation of post-War white masculinity? Or will his administration represent the embodiment of something very old and very new about how empires end, civilizations crumble, and democratic self-governance shades into ethno-chauvinism, autocracy, and eventual collapse? Will terrible events in the future force us to look back on this period in the same way we gasp at the complacency and self-satisfaction of Europe in the first decade of the twentieth century? Or will in thirty years our willful blindness to population increase, resource scarcity, demographic shifts, climate change, and the breakdown of international comity and cooperation be so self-evident, that if 2017 is remembered, it will be as one of many years of denial, numerous failures of public policy, and societal inaction that revealed clearly the shortcomings of our species?

As it is, we're too close in time and space to make a determination as to what this man (who is unnamed by me throughout this work) *means* for the Republic.

During the 2016 presidential campaign, the Republican nominee said he'd put people to work. As the many despairing screeds, anxious opinion editorials, admonitory books, furious blogs, and second-by-second freak-out postings on social media demonstrate, in this case, at least, he fulfilled his promise. *The Trumpiad* is one such labor—if not for love or money, then at least in a passionate and dogged commitment to the quixotic, anachronistic, and esoteric.

Conceived in the spirit of Lord Byron's *Don Juan*, and with nods to Alexander Pope's *Dunciad*, Samuel Butler's *Hudibras*, and even *Byrne* by Anthony Burgess, *The Trumpiad* is my preposterous panjandrum, loaded with explosive feelings, subterranean rumblings, *de profundis* howlings, and exhortations befitting the Biblical prophets, about the man, the country of which I became a citizen in 2013, and the election of 2016 in which I cast my first vote for president.

As my illustrious and talented forebears in the genre demonstrated much more ably than I, the mock-heroic verse epic offers a way to combine the contemporary and banal with the ancient and high-minded, using language both hifalutin and demotic. The rhyme scheme I've chosen (*abababcc*, or *ottava rima*, employed by Byron in *Don Juan*) provides pith and apothegmatic irony (in the use of a concluding couplet) and presents the possibility of discursive and even absurd rhyming patterns in the six lines that precede it. Those two extra lines pull the quatrain apart enough to let lightheartedness and gassy excess in, add a little piquancy to a bland phrase or, as W. S. Gilbert so incisively put it in *The Mikado*, to "give verisimilitude to an otherwise bald and unconvincing narrative."

Unlike the more considered and considerable works that were my models, I decided to risk immediate irrelevance by writing each canto in the days leading to the month that would follow. Thus, the thirty-one stanzas of Canto I were composed in December 2016 (with material purloined from earlier writings) and published online as January 2017. I managed to continue this regimen until October, when events (and life) caught up with me. Throughout the year, immediate occurrences, and books, films, and other items, drew me into larger reflections about the times we live in and the country that, as of 2017, I had lived in for half my life.

Unlike the online version of this work, I've been less assiduous in this printed form in offering synonyms for or explanations of unfamiliar words. Some of the atmospherics of the mock-heroic are generated by the author's (and reader's) reveling in orotundity and obscurantism, and I have inhaled deeply those heady vapors. I do, however, parse literary and other references in footnotes that, it should be admitted, are also deliberately fustian, frequently unhelpful, and occasionally rude. At the end of the book, I provide brief summaries of the *dramatis personae* and related affairs that constituted the pantomime of the first year of the administration—as well as some of the mythological and literary characters who make occasional appearances throughout.

To an observer, particularly someone who considers him- or herself a conservative, the reactions in *The Trumpiad* to events and personalities no doubt will appear conventionally liberal—born out of the assumptions and prejudices that many "high-information," graduate-class urbanites held (and continue to hold) about the president and his voters: assumptions and prejudices reinforced within our social-media, regional, and other bubbles. I certainly don't deny this critique. In my defense, in 2017 I exposed myself to opinions and judgments more right- and left-wing than my own, while allowing myself the opportunity to console or depress myself with the fact that I was similarly dismayed by how President Bush came to office in 2000, and how *he* conducted himself during his first year. I'm sure someone could have said the same thing about every preceding president. However, I do think time will reveal that the forty-fifth president of the United States manifested uniquely awful and destructive qualities that conservatives with a conscience noted, protested, and revolted against—or, at least, *should* have done.

One final observation. During the year, I found myself immersed in thinking about how our current politics—obsessed with minutiae and the latest outrage, distracted by the horse race and confused or ill-informed about policy, full of grandstanding and purity tests—could possibly cope with the huge, systemic changes underway: from technology that is rendering industrial manual labor obsolete, to the rise of global authoritarianism, to the wholly inadequate responses to climate change. *The Trumpiad* expresses that anxiety while adding to the fog that clouds the kind of farsighted resilience that will be necessary over the next half-century if we are not to descend into massive civil unrest, global conflict, or environmental catastrophe.

An Additional Note on the Verse

It would have been beyond my skills as a versifier to have produced 365 eight-line stanzas without the liberal use of enjambment (where the sense of the sentence is carried over from one line to the next) or letting a concluding polysyllabic word's rhyme fall on the first or second syllable—as in the first two stanzas of Canto I. I revised the cantos throughout the year, but only to correct typographical errors and change false rhymes or rhymes that were in British English (Received Pronunciation) to standard American. I also removed the occasionally repetitive word construction. At times, I know, I strain to keep the iambic rhythm, but I've tried to give the syllabic construction a spoken feel: in other words, "our" and "real" are rendered disyllabically usually, as is "every"; however, there are many exceptions, and my advice is to go with the flow of ordinary speech whenever you can.

That the content remained basically the same is not down to any astonishing powers of prognostication I may possess or even to dumb luck. Unfortunately, the problems of systemic violence, racism, misogyny, and political inertia and posturing existed before "45" was sworn in and will remain after he is, with any luck, kicked out. Perhaps his coming into office and the manner of his leaving it will galvanize the nation to address these embedded problems. I'm not holding my breath.

Canto I
January 2017

I

In olden days, a writer with pretension
    To voice his people's hopes in smooth hexameter,
Would make a case for poetic ascension
    By laying down an ode or epigrammata
Before composing something with dimension,
    For risk he'd be exposed as a rank amateur.
Why show you're just another two-bit schemer
And what's more do it in *ottava rima*?

II

But there's no time for artistic probation:
    The game's afoot, time ripe, the need is now.
The fate of the Republic's the vexation:
    Whether we last through these four years, and how.
When a sham ignoramus runs the nation,
    Who cares if I'm sufficiently high-brow
To catch the wretched *agon* of the times
Successfully in Tasso's piquant rhymes?

Hexameter. The form favored by classical poets writing heroic verse.
Ottava rima. See *Author's Note*.
Agon. The Ancient Greek term that means "contest" or "struggle," and from which we
    get the word *agony*.
Tasso. For a glossary of names, see *Dramatis Personae* at the back of the book.

III

Lord Byron knew the mixture well: *Don Juan*
    Incorporates the seemly and the seamy.
And per the era, I venture a new one
    Should be both sanctimonious and steamy.
To tenderize the shock of knowing who won
    And help us chew, then somewhat tart and creamy
Must be my verse: to catch the *zeitgeist*'s mood
Demands the euphuistic and the crude.

IV

It's usual in this type of composition
    To issue forth a ringing invocation:
A call to arms, a plea for a commission
    To bind the wounds; locate a lofty station
From which to proffer a worthy petition
    Or lift the veil upon a desecration.
I need a spot where I can coalesce
Each bilious outflow in one putrid mess.

V

O soft Gowanus: issue forth your scents
    To cleanse my verse; your waters rank and deep
Diffuse my fetid spewing; in your dense
    Alembic boil each noxious phrasing, steep
Within your nacreous current each offense,
    And turn from dross to gold this steaming heap

Don Juan. Byron's pronunciation rhymes with "new one."
Euphuistic. Elaborate, precocious, and particularly precious form of writing. The adjective derives from *Euphues: The Anatomy of Wit*, an English prose romance by John Lily, published in 1578, which is particularly flowery.
Gowanus refers to a neighborhood and canal in South Brooklyn, which the Environmental Protection Agency designated for environmental remediation in 2010. It has been heavily polluted by oil and heavy metals for at least a century.
Alembic. A tube employed in alchemy.
Nacreous. The color of mother-of-pearl.

That like compost builds life. Is it obscene
To call on you, my flush-full Hippocrene?

VI

Where are you KENTILE sign, whose lambent beams
    Once shone upon the sludge-filled sites below?
Where are the slicks you lit, the oil-tar seams,
    The bodies swaying in the undertow
Of the canal? Bless my cloacal memes,
    Which rise above South Brooklyn's dirty glow,
Drivers who contemplate tranquility
When stuck in traffic on the BQE.

VII

Muse, cross the bridges: Newark's meadows sweet,
    Old Cleveland's groves, the springs of Buffalo,
Descant upon the passing of Main Street,
    Now empty, once full not so long ago.
Detroit shall echo, Gary shall repeat
    That what was manufactured is no mo':
For why spend time in genuine creation
When wealth is made through idle speculation?

Flush-full Hippocrene. A play on the sewage that pours into the canal and line 16 of
  John Keats' "Ode to a Nightingale," in which the poet hymns the clear spring of Mt.
  Helicon, which in classical times was considered sacred to the Muses. The canal's
  flushing system is often broken.
KENTILE sign. The sign for Kentile floor tiles, first erected in 1949, was taken down in 2014.
Bodies swaying. The Gowanus Canal is rumored to be where organized crime disposes of
  the bodies. It's unlikely that the bodies would sway for long before dissolving.
Cloacal. Pertaining to a bodily sewer.
BQE. The Brooklyn–Queens Expressway, which runs through the neighborhood, is a
  byword for traffic congestion.
Newark's meadows sweet. These towns' bucolic appellations are ironic: all are notorious
  for their pollution and industrial blight.
Is no mo'. The use of the shorthand refers back to "Mo'town," the name given to Detroit
  as the capital of the American motor industry.

VIII

Look! How we supplicants the levers yank
    And buttons push (the gamblers' Vitus' dance);
Or rub the lotto genie and so bank
    The future on the one-in-a-million chance!
Deposits going south, stocks in the tank,
    The houses worthless. And yet, in a trance,
We reckon if we placed just one more bet
We'd magically dissolve our unpaid debt.

IX

Speak, Prophet, let each narcissistic byte
    Decode the bibble-babble of this age.
Dismantle every cable droid, indict
    Each billion-dollar suit, and turn your rage
Upon the posing proxies that each night
    Pour forth the toxic gas that drives the gauge
That measures book advances, honoraria,
And gobs of cash spat forth in faux hysteria.

X

Descry, O Instant Messenger, the stores
    And houses boarded up, the vacant lots
And men who cluster at the corner, scores
    To settle or trace up arms, the easy shots
That have no consequence—for all the doors
    Have long since been foreclosed on. Join the dots,
You gamers, for the people are in hock
For taking and not taking enough stock.

Vitus' dance. St. Vitus' dance, or rapid, uncoordinated actions.
Speak. Verses VII–IX were written in 2009, in the wake of the financial crisis of 2007–08.
    However, they could easily refer to the deindustrialized wasteland of many parts of the
    Rust Belt and Appalachia in 2016 and 2017.
Bibble-babble. See William Shakespeare's *Twelfth Night*, 4, ii, 103.

XI

Direct your gaze toward the gilded suite
    Within the Tower; settling on the sofa,
Consider how the bully deigns to meet
    Each sycophantic leech and fawning gopher,
How much he smirks as on their knees they bleat
    For work, pretending he is not a loafer.
As long as they're on good terms with the bruiser,
They think that he won't shame them as a loser.

XII

A puffed-up peacock, scabrous popinjay;
    Falstaff without the grace or sack or wit;
A loathsome skeeve, a spawn of Rabelais;
    A thin-skinned and vainglorious hypocrite,
Is the Commander of the U.S.A.
    Revisit that when next you take a shit.
Let tumble from your bowels into the pan
Just what you think about this wretched man.

XIII

"But wait!" I hear you say, "he's now our chief,
    And sixty million folks can't be mistaken.
We needed change, and Hillary's a thief,
    And now the ruling classes are left shaken,
Because of their presumptuousness. Your beef
    Is just sour grapes. And soon you will awaken
In a U.S. of A. that's rightly ours,
In which we'll wield full presidential powers."

Tower. The building, on Fifth Avenue, between 57th and 58th streets in Manhattan, named after the real-estate tycoon, where he interviewed Cabinet members between his election on November 8, 2016, and Inauguration Day, January 20, 2017.
Scabrous. Salacious.
Popinjay. A vain person.
Sack. Archaic term for wine. The current occupant of the White House is a teetotaler.
Skeeve. A sleazy individual.

XIV

My answer to these claims of right is "No."
No to accepting that this harlequin
Has any right to strut and primp and crow.
I see no cause to offer him my chin
To punch. This bald-faced Braggadocio
Will not go underided. If I sin
It would be in not being hard enough
Upon the flaunting, pompous piece of fluff.

XV

"Good riddance to Obama!" comes the cry,
"The Muslim, godless stooge, the Communist,
The enemy within, the Kenyan spy,
The interloping, false-flag terrorist,
With his transgendered wife." A desperate try
To stigmatize a couple who'll be missed.
Your smears were never facts, but fever dreams:
Unlike your man; for he is as he seems.

XVI

What standards the Obamas had to meet!
They couldn't be angry, browbeat or defame,
Or marry twice or thrice. They couldn't tweet
Insults or obloquy, affront or shame.
Their kids had to be kind and smart and sweet,
Michelle compassionate and without blame:
They always had to leave a good impression
And not commit a solitary transgression.

Harlequin. A joker in pantomime.
Good riddance. The right called Barack and Michelle Obama many epithets (several contradictory), and concocted extraordinary fantasies—including that Obama was gay, Michelle was a man or transgendered, and that their two daughters were adopted.
False-flag. The term used to describe an event a shadowy (usually governmental) agency has staged to redirect attention from an illegal or oppressive action by the state.
Obloquy. Verbal abuse.

XVII

And now we are confronted with this Nero
    Who'll fiddle as the planet burns: his pride
And vanity unmatched; the perfect hero
    For this land, where misconduct is denied,
Compunction shunned, and where a total zero
    Can justify state torture, and deride
As quisling crybabies those who attempt
To offer another vision. What contempt!

XVIII

Is it not weird he has no hinterland?
    No book or film or play that moved his soul,
No cultural lodestars, neither small nor grand,
    That left him vulnerable or made him whole?
It seems that he's mere surface (and it's tanned),
    A world of flash and shimmer, without toll:
No weight of loss or sorrow or regret.
Good Lord, he doesn't even have a pet!

XIX

What will he do when he is called to grieve
    When natural disaster strikes the nation?
One-forty characters will not relieve
    The pain of lives destroyed; nor adoration,
Disdain, or ridicule help us believe
    The leader knows the sting of deprivation.
When hugs need to be given, will he reel?
Or, arms extended, will he cop a feel?

Compunction. Guilt and scruple.
Quisling. A traitor, from Vidkun Quisling (1887–1945), a pro-Nazi leader of Norway.
Lodestars. Guiding principles.
One-forty characters. The number of characters allowed for sending a message ("tweet")
    on the social-media platform Twitter. Recently expanded to two hundred and eighty.

XX

More worryingly still, when terror hits,
    As it most surely will, will he react
Judiciously, advisedly? Or blitz
    A city, region, country when attacked
To prove his manliness? Or blow to bits
    Each treaty, bloc, agreement, and compact:
Provide the terrorists with what they need
To fill the beds once more at Walter Reed?

XXI

Perhaps the Prez will be as disengaged
    As George Bush was in his first months: content
To hit the golf course and become enraged
    At *SNL*, while trying to foment
Some phony crisis so he's not upstaged
    By the dull busyness of government.
He'll sit counting his future bucks and cents
And hand over the Executive to Pence.

XXII

The danger is he'll think he knows it all:
    Filling the airwaves with his contradictions.
There'll be perpetual conflict, and in thrall
    To self-lit conflagrations and the fictions,
Distracted by the thrill of daily brawl,
    We'll exhaust outrage nursing our afflictions.
Meanwhile the Congress will pass legislation
To end the federal administration.

Walter Reed. The national medical center that receives and treats U.S. soldiers wounded in combat.

SNL. *Saturday Night Live,* a comedy-sketch show on NBC Television, which first began airing in 1975. It ridiculed the G.O.P. nominee relentlessly throughout 2016 and 2017.

XXIII

One tenders hope that the judicial branch
    Will work to halt congressional overreach;
That genuine conservatives will blanch
    At efforts to undermine freedoms of speech,
Assembly, privacy; will salve or stanch
    The wounds inflicted; or they'll block the breach
Made in the wall dividing church and state,
And protect the defenseless against hate.

XXIV

One might repose some trust, if just a flicker,
    That senators will act with gravitas,
And seek out common ground to act (don't snicker!).
    If not, then frankly it might come to pass
That Jefferson's republic (here's the kicker),
    Will fold before this truculent jackass:
And what we will be left with will be amurcous
Game shows of unrelenting bread and circus.

XXV

Yet what about the notion that the chump
    Will (at last!) shake things up, and, by upending,
Return some power to the people, pump
The economy with infrastructure spending,
And catapult us from this so-called slump
    Into a future glory never-ending?
Well, yes, he *might*—except that he's abstaining
From every promise that he made campaigning.

Amurcous. Stinky.

XXVI

What makes this flagrant treachery more galling
    Is how he savors playing us for fools.
Beyond his bombast, tantrums, and name-calling
    His goal seems only to dispense with rules
To allow infractions even more appalling.
    It's obvious that he considers mules
The folks who voted for him, suckers all,
Stick figures scrawled upon his bullshit Wall.

XXVII

The coal and steel jobs are not coming back,
    Obamacare's repeal has no replacement;
The Wall will not be built, and every claque
    Is lining up for inside perks. Abasement
Will be complete when every stooge and hack
    Is settled into every job and space meant
For those who care for their agency's mission,
Instead of beating it into contrition.

XXVIII

So now we wait to see what fate will show.
    The U.S.A. has been through worse—got through
The Civil War, slaveholding, the Alamo,
    Pearl Harbor, My Lai, Watergate; and grew

Bullshit Wall. The plan to build a physical wall over the entire length of the U.S.–Mexican border proved popular with the Republican base during the 2016 campaign.

Obamacare. The name given to the Affordable Care Act, the signature piece of legislation of the Obama presidency.

Civil War. The Civil War (1861–65) caused the deaths of around 620,000 soldiers and hundreds of thousands more from disease.

Alamo. The 1836 slaughter at the Alamo mission, in what would become Texas.

Pearl Harbor. The bombing of the port in Hawaii territory by Japan on December 7, 1941 brought the U.S. into World War II.

My Lai. The village where in 1968 U.S. soldiers massacred hundreds of unarmed civilians during the Vietnam War.

Following 9/11. Even so
That better days await might not be true:
Reliant on exclusion and amnesia,
Dispensed through a collective anesthesia.

XXIX

Oh man! I hope that we are proven wrong,
And suddenly he is magnanimous:
Reforms the prisons, builds the roads, makes strong
The economy (and does it without fuss),
Returns power to where it should belong,
While not throwing the weak under the bus,
And, though admitting that he can be crude,
Ensures that only rich people are screwed.

XXX

So now we wait for the Inauguration,
The senses frayed, and hearts and souls a-flutter,
What will he say to calm a frazzled nation?
What soaring rhetoric will this man utter?
Will he, at last, ascend to meet the station
To which he aspired, or will he simply mutter
A few pat phrases from the autocue
Before attacking his latest bugaboo?

XXXI

What will it be? Four years of garbled tweets,
Of grievance, surliness, dissimulation?
Four years of protest marches in the streets,
Met each night with a pettish lucubration?

Watergate. The break-in at Democratic National Committee headquarters in the Watergate complex in Washington, D.C. in 1972, ultimately led to the resignation of President Richard Nixon (under threat of impeachment) in 1974.

9/11. The terrorist attacks on New York City and Washington, D.C. by Al-Qaeda on September 11, 2001.

Pettish lucubration. A childish and petulant piece of maudlin writing.

Of dirt (financial and between the sheets),
   Corruption, filth, and misappropriation;
Or something else? Distinction or disgrace?
We'll find out soon enough; so, watch this space.

Canto II

February 2017

I

Where are the songs of Spring? (You may well ask.)
    Where weeds in wheels shoot long and lovely and lush.
The darling bud's not ready for the task,
    The lark ascending but a darkling thrush.
The smell of dread's cloaked by a facial mask,
    And hectic cheeks rosy with flu's first blush:
We raise a cry, given our president,
"Now is the winter of our discontent."

II

It's only been two weeks, and madness brews!
    The Constitution creeks and sighs and buckles.
The lawyers have descended! Talks of coups,
    Secret cabals, and gangs may give you chuckles
But this seems scary-true to me. A fuse
    Is lit: I counsel, "Get out your brass knuckles."
For something quite explosive has begun
And there'll be street-fighting before it's done.

Where are the songs of spring? The following works are referenced in this stanza: John Keats' "Ode to Autumn," line 23; Gerard Manley Hopkins' "Spring," line 2; William Shakespeare's Sonnet XVIII, line 3; George Meredith's "The Lark Ascending"; Thomas Hardy's "The Darkling Thrush"; and Shakespeare's *Richard III*, I, i, 1.

III

I know last canto's tone was too threnodic.
 But like so many, I was out of humor.
I sought for major strains, something melodic,
 Yet what were sounded were the bells of doom; a
Long, plangent, ululatory, spasmodic,
 Dyspeptic groan at the malignant tumor
That's formed within the body politic,
And hasn't been excised yet. Sick, O sick!

IV

Therefore, instead of taking medication,
 Let me recall a *topos* from the ages:
A listing of the heroes of the nation,
 No longer here, but who now fill the pages
Of history books. They reached the highest station,
 And by the lesson of their lives, these sages
Reveal to us it might not be as bad
As it might seem in this dark season. Sad!

V

Picture a man uneasy in his skin,
 Of awkward twitches, blatant paranoia,
Without a friend, but enemies within,
 Who craves respect from those he loathes; destroyer
Of an elite that will not let him in;
 Whose angst is that a congressman or lawyer
Will strip from him the one thing he gets kicks in:
That's power. I refer to Richard Nixon.

Threnodic. Dirge-like.
Ululatory. Wailing and mournful.
Sick, O Sick. See Shakespeare's *King Lear*, V, iii, 96.
Topos. A commonplace or archetypal rhetorical construction.
Sad! A *topos* frequently employed by 45 in his tweets.

VI

Is Tricky Dick not the progenitor?
    Think of it: subterfuge, plots, half-baked theories,
The all-consuming need to settle a score,
    The exposés, the leaks, an endless series
Of depositions, cover-ups, and more,
    Leaving the world astonished at the sheer ease
With which one man can macerate the nation
Unless allowed to freebase adulation.

VII

Recall the Hardings and their Teapot Domes,
    And Wilson's resurrection of the Klan;
The bought-and-paid-for Gilded Age's gnomes
    Who helped the rich grow richer; and the span
Van Buren to Buchanan. Thoughtful tomes
    Indict their many frauds and failures. Can
We locate in the list an Anglo-Saxon
More cruel than the bloody Andrew Jackson?

VIII

I venture not. Yet mediocrities
    (Like Major Major) need a sinecure.
They, too, seek graft and love perquisites!
    How else will cocky layabouts ensure

Macerate. Crush and tear apart.
Hardings. The administration of President Warren Harding was known for its scandals, including a bribery scheme at Teapot Dome in Wyoming in 1923.
Wilson's resurrection. In 1915, President Woodrow Wilson invited film director D. W. Griffith to show *The Birth of a Nation* at the White House. The film's positive depiction of the Ku Klux Klan (KKK) enabled the terrorist organization to grow in the U.S.
Gilded Age. During the period roughly from 1870–1900, presidents failed to stop the massive concentration of wealth among so-called robber barons.
Van Buren to Buchanan. The eight presidents from Martin van Buren to James Buchanan were unable or unwilling to grapple with the causes of the Civil War.
Sinecure. A make-do job for a political favorite.

That others do the work so they can squeeze
    Into their schedule one more victory tour?
It's fun to spend one's time before adoring
Crowds chanting your name. All the rest is boring!

IX

This man, therefore, is not an aberration.
    He seems that way because we have forgot
How much the past reveals the amputation
    Of truth from how we dream we were: the rot
Of sharecropping and lynching, segregation,
    Of Joe McCarthy, tenements, the lot
Of native peoples and the broken pacts:
These are not myths or misconstrued; they're facts.

X

What if he's ill, not merely solipsistic?
    What if he cannot function without crisis?
You sense he's desperate to go ballistic
    And take thousands of troops to war with ISIS;
Inflate his chest and pose in a fascistic
    Homage to Mussolini, which is why this
Scenario's so weird. I ask again:
What if the U.S. president's insane?

XI

It started at the Correspondents' Dinner
    When President Obama—who of late

ISIS. One of the names for Islamic State, an insurgent Islamist terrorist group that took
    over, occupied, and declared a caliphate, in a large part of Syria and Iraq between
    2014 and 2017. By the end of 2017, ISIS's territories had largely been reconquered by
    Iraqi, Kurdish, and Syrian forces.
Correspondents' Dinner. A black-tie dinner for members of the media, celebrities, and
    politicians, where the president traditionally gives a humorous speech. The one in
    question took place in 2011.

This man had been asserting was a sinner
    For not releasing his certificate
Of birth, and claiming he would soon begin a
    Phishing trip to make sure he was innate—
Determined at the banquet with the accuser
To have a little fun with his abuser.

XII

It turned out that the "tough" investigator
    Discovered that he didn't like to see
The truth about himself. The fabricator
    Resolved to run for office. History
Will demonstrate that this manipulator
    Decided to destroy the powers that be
Not out of care for ordinary folk
But just because he couldn't take a joke.

XIII

The trouble is he's not a merry pranker
    Who yearns to punk and make his trifling plays.
He thrives on turmoil, enmity, and rancor,
    Thrills in deflection, falsehood, and malaise.
In English parlance, he's a frigging wanker
    Who kicks the sticks from old people, and preys
Upon the fragile. If he acts the thug,
He thinks, no one will see under the rug.

Certificate. The current incumbent of the Oval Office was instrumental in raising questions about whether Obama was actually born in Hawaii and not outside the U.S. (for instance, in Kenya, the birthplace of Obama's father), thus making him ineligible to be president.

Phishing. A form of cyber scam or spamming that attempts to gain sensitive private information. Despite the TV entertainer's claims that his investigators were uncovering evidence proving Obama was not born in Hawaii, no proof was ever found. Obama ultimately displayed his birth certificate in 2010.

Frigging wanker. The redundancies in the phrase suggest excessive masturbation.

XIV

Talking of which, please tell me what's that carpet
  That sits atop his head? A dormant rat?
A shiny coprolite dug from a tar pit?
  A grouchy and albino Maine Coon cat?
The decomposing body of a varmit,
  Or golden *guano* from a loose-bowelled bat?
It looks like someone piled on wet spaghetti
And dried it to resemble a small Yeti.

XV

Now I don't like to dwell in negativity:
  I'm mostly Mr. Sunshine, happy camper.
If leaning to the good is my proclivity
  Then surely (without being a rubber stamper)
I should say something nice. For expressivity
  That's only doom and gloom will be a damper
And make us want to clasp our knees and rock.
So I'll reframe these features that I mock.

XVI

O weave supreme, a glorious filigree
  Of cultivated strands, metallic weft,
Frozen by gel, embalmed through chemistry,
  Each follicle effulgent: right and left
Can marvel at the stylist's topiary,
  That threaded so few hairs into such heft.
Bald Opportunity is most dismayed
To see his single hair in that blond braid.

Coprolite. Fossilized dung.
Varmit. Alternative form of "varmint."
Guano. Bat excreta.
Effulgent. Shining like lightning.
Bald Opportunity. In Greek mythology, Kairos, the figure of Opportunity or Time, is
  often depicted as possessing only a single hair on his head.

XVII

Upholstered fleece: an auric monument
    To everything he's hungered for since birth;
A cover for his failures (youth misspent,
    Failed marriages, the bankruptcies). It's worth
In sleek and contoured moldings that augment
    His dome to him is much more than the mirth
That falls upon its lustrous sward like dew
And polishes his barefaced self anew.

XVIII

And what about those gestures so balletic?
    The forefinger and thumb (perverted *mudra*)
Bespeaking . . . what? Precision? Truth emetic?
    The prissy cynicism of his *sudra*
That highlights how easily the bathetic
    Can hide the fact that an almighty budra
Is going to be levied on your ass!
Don't be confused by postures that look crass.

XIX

O brazen sybarite, whose farouche moue
    Puckers with such fastidious disdain.
Not even Blanche DuBois could swoon and stew
    In such "melodramatic diva" vein.
Carnival barker, breathy ingénue,
    Both Susan Alexander and Charles Kane:
Not to be ostentatiously ungallant,
I must say, "Exit right; you have no talent."

Auric. Golden.
Mudra. A sacred arrangement of fingers on the hand in Hinduism and Buddhism.
Sudra. Caste or class in Hinduism.
Bathetic. Anti-climactic and banal, for the purposes of comedy.
Budra. Urban slang for ass-kicking.
Sybarite. Named after Sybaris, a town in ancient Greece, known for its love of pleasure
    and indulgence.
Farouche moue. A sullen pout.

XX

What honeyed words shall we say of Melania?
    That she's a sylph in bondage to Silenus?
Or like the accurséd fairy queen Titania
    Enamored of an ass? A marbled Venus
Carved by jealous Pygmalion? An ania
    To a flame? The sheath that covers up his penis
And offers him the semblance of propriety
To make sure it's not unmasked in society?

XXI

Observing her pinched features, fixed and strained,
    You sense that something has gone wrong. As if
What, years ago, she bargained for has drained
    The joy from her. And like a living GIF
She's trapped in the same motions; every pained,
    Thin smile; her slender body taut and stiff:
These show she knows and worries that her beau
Will one day say, "You're fired," and she'll go.

XXII

Where is the joshing, where the amorous ease,
    The warmth that comes from knowing that your guy
Has reached the top? I wonder, did he squeeze
    Her hand that first night, look her in the eye
And say that he was sorry for the sleaze,
    But that man was no more? That he would try
To be someone of whom she could be proud,
With whom she could stand resolute, unbowed?

Ania. A kind of moth.

GIF. A graphics interchange format. In animated form, the GIF expresses a repeated gesture, often to comic effect.

"You're fired". The signature send-off line uttered by the real-estate tycoon during his multi-year engagement as the star of the TV show, *The Apprentice*.

XXIII

Yet there she is, untouched and unadored,
    Who walks behind him as he strides ahead.
Locked in her ornate cage, depressed and bored
    Out of her skull, each day is filled with dread
At what he'll say or do next. Her accord
    For staying with him's ultimately led
To being First Lady and the people's house
And yet she wakes still married to a louse.

XXIV

Unlike the elder children, with their shrewd
    Accommodations to the Chief, their sire,
She and her son look haunted and subdued.
    What does she know, what has she seen transpire
Within those marbled walls? Did she conclude
    That it was best to shrink back and retire
Rather than be herself and thereby cross
The man she once loved, who is now her boss?

XXV

Has she awoken in the dark of night
    And wandered to the living room to find
His jowly mien wan in the cellphone's light
    Or staring at the TV screens? Do kind
Hands settle on his shoulders: "It's not right,"
    She says, "they're merely messing with your mind.
Let them alone and come to bed, my sweet.
It doesn't matter. You've no need to tweet"?

XXVI

Does he reply, "You'll never understand.
  I cannot let them have the final word.
I've never lost. I always win. Command
  And others act—that's me. No little turd
With half a brain will beat me. I demand
  Complete respect"? So, by reason unspurred,
(While she retreats, knowing she's tried her best),
Do his two stubby fingers do the rest?

XXVII

So much for being nice! I must admit
  I find it hard to separate the man
From *that* office in which he sits. The shit
  Is flying but has not yet hit the fan,
And yet we wade through ordure. Piles of it:
  A vast lake from Orlando to Spokane.
And every movement, statement, and booboo
Bears undisputed vestiges of poo.

XXVIII

So, no, I won't go high when they go low.
  (Apologies, Michelle!) What sorts of scold
Would Swift or Joseph Heller or Thiong'o
  Be if they meekly did as they were told
By those in power? When the ill winds blow
  You open up your cheeks and blast, tenfold,
Ripostes both sobering and pedagogical,
Or, failing that, overtly scatological.

(Apologies Michelle!). Michelle Obama told the audience at the 2016 Democratic National Convention to respond to critics thus: "When they go low, we go high."

Canto III

March 2017

I

In epics, usually at their very heart,
  The plot stops and the hero, marked by fate,
Encounters a Parnassian whose art
  The poet thinks incomparable. The great
Wordsmith displays a tableau that, from start
  To end, unfurls a pageant of the state,
With warriors both mythic and historical,
And women who are plainly allegorical.

II

This interlude's intended to attest
  To those who thought you just a Grub Street hack,
That you've a right to be among the best,
  And that you don't care if they're talking smack

In epics. This canto was inspired by an op-ed by Maureen Dowd in *The New York Times* on February 18, 2017, in which she described the vices in 45's head. Odysseus and Aeneas visit the Underworld in *Odyssey*, Book XI and *Aeneid*, Book VI, respectively.

Parnassian. In Greek mythology, Mt. Parnassus is the home of Apollo and the Muses. The poet I'm mainly thinking of is Virgil in Dante's *Divina Commedia*.

Grub Street. An impoverished area of London populated by writers, and satirized by Alexander Pope (1688–1744) in his *Dunciad*.

About you—you know you're not like the rest,
>For Destiny's fair winds are at your back.
You are the voice and conscience of the age:
Pretenders will be forced to leave the stage!

III

If nothing else, conning this entr'acte
>Gives you a chance to prove you've got the chops:
Skewering enemies, displaying tact
>With those who may go either way, and props
To those who are your friends—for now. Thus, packed
>With figures (in both senses), such name-drops
With any luck might last for centuries,
Although we know there are no guarantees.

IV

That time has come, dear reader: let's descend
>Into the depths of Hades, where the Styx
Meanders through the Tartaran gloom. Attend!
>The lost ones wailing at our politics;
The anguish of the Founders at the end
>Of the Republic. Even dreary Nyx
Pleads for a glint of lightness to set free
The souls of Uncle Sam and Liberty.

V

These two were last seen at the Inauguration.
>They'd come from sleeping in a cardboard shack
Near the Potomac, to cheer on the nation
>As it changed leaders. But their jaws fell slack

Entr'acte. Interlude between acts in a play.
Props. Slang for "credit" or "respect."
With figures (in both senses). In the sense of a bodily form and a rhetorical "figure."
Potomac. The main river of Washington, D.C.

At the new president's disinformation.
     With shattered hearts they wandered slowly back
And that night gave their country up for lost.
They sought out Charon, paid their dues, and crossed.

VI

How sad they seem! How gaunt, how wan, how worn!
     The flaming torch that she had once upheld
Extinguished; his stovepipe tattered and torn;
     The passion in his piercing eyes now quelled;
And facial muscles sallow, limp, forlorn,
     As if from Eden they had been expelled.
On seeing them, so downcast, frail, and weak,
I summon up my wits and start to speak.

VII

I call to them, "O Lady Liberty
     And Uncle Sam, had you waited a day,
You would have stood among a shining sea
     Of people of all colors, straight and gay,
Befitting what it means to be the Free
     Of this fair land." But they wander away,
Not hearing what I cry. I shake my head:
It's not that easy comforting the dead.

VIII

My eyes search for the Sybil for this mission:
     Who might I—poetaster, versifier—

The flaming torch. Lady Liberty's extinguished torch was the cover of the February 13 & 20, 2017 edition of *The New Yorker*.

As if from Eden. I have in mind William Blake's illustration of Adam and Eve's expulsion from Paradise for John Milton's *Paradise Lost*.

You would have stood. On January 21, 2017, a day after the Inauguration, hundreds of thousands gathered in Washington, D.C., in the Women's March on Washington.

Shining sea. A phrase taken from the song "God Bless America," by Irving Berlin.

Ask as a guide for such a composition?
Nor Virgil, Hermes, Homer, nor the lyre
Of Orpheus are in my range; my edition
Needs a cut-price Calliope to inspire.
Without blinking an eye (for I'm not proud),
I summon the etheric Maureen Dowd.

IX

Behold she manifests herself! Her retinue
Are twin putti, Irreverence and Snark,
And weird sisters, Smirk and Snide and Rue.
The five give me the side eye, and remark,
"How strange it is that a rube such as you,
Would have the chutzpah, gumption, or the spark
To call forth such as one as She, whose irony
Is wasted on a putz who thinks he's Byron-y."

X

"Silence," commands La Dowd, "for this poor fool
Must needs receive a vision; a charade
That I shall place before him that will school
Him in lampoon and farce; a cavalcade
Of failings and defects. For ridicule
Must scatter the grotesque harlequinade
Of ogres that goosestep within the pate
Of that man who is now the head of state."

XI

She lifts her arms, and suddenly a cloud
Descends. I blink and stare: before my face
Deplorables effuse from the black shroud

Etheric. In the esoteric Western tradition, the subtle body.
Putti. Cherubs in Renaissance art.
Weird sisters. See William Shakespeare's *Macbeth*, 1, iii, 33.
Deplorables. In 2016, the Democratic Party's presidential nominee, Hillary Clinton, described some of her opponent's supporters as "a basket of deplorables."

Of deepest darkness and take up their place.
I cannot but admire how Maureen Dowd
    Can conjure a cabal of such disgrace
As these atrocious phantoms. There they cluster:
A murderers' row of perfidy and bluster.

XII

First, Insecurity: twitching and wincing,
    Ranting about his ratings and fake news;
His arms flap as he tries to be convincing
    At how much he's admired by the Jews.
Yet all the while, between the camp and mincing,
    He's scared someone will say that this king's trews
Are non-existent, and the only clothing
He shrouds himself with are terror and loathing.

XIII

Next, Insincerity: homunculus,
    A fawning, two-faced fraud, fair-weather chum.
So filled with fat lies is this incubus,
    He floats free of the real. This pond scum
Is so infected and befouled with puss
    That he makes those who know him sick and numb:
For there is yet no surefire antidote
To remedy ventripotence and bloat.

XIV

Third in this wretched chain is Victimhood,
    Sullen and mewling, whining, pouting, glum.

Fake news. A standard talking-point of the right regarding the mainstream media's
    promotion of and concentration on stories perceived to be partisan.
Trews. English slang for trousers or pants.
Homunculus. A miniature representation of a human being.
Incubus. A malevolent being.
Ventripotence. Possessing a bloated stomach.

"Why can't I get my own way? I'll be good,
    I promise," is the falsehood that this bum
Whimpers and snivels. "I'm misunderstood."
    Yet Victimhood's sly grin shows he's not dumb.
If you cross him he'll really put the boot in,
Either with goons or with his great pal Putin.

XV

Then twin sisters, Bullying and Suspicion:
    Mean girls who detest those whom they admire;
Their shoulders cold, they seek total submission
    From those they think might have their measure; fire
The talented and worthy. A condition
    Of being a cool kid is you conspire
Against all comers: for it's very clear
That if they can't love you, at least they fear.

XVI

That shade rubbing his hands is Calculation:
    His task to uproot Kindness and Largesse;
To work without respite to spike inflation
    And expand Insincerity's vile mess.
There's Self-delusion (way above his station)
    And clinging on despite lack of success.
And leading them in chants, replete with bile,
Is Gall, his mug sprayed with an unctuous smile.

XVII

The rest of them are lost within the herd
    Of gluttons and con-artists, a great crowd
Of flies that swarm the Vices. A huge turd
    From Egomania expels a cloud

Unctuous. Oily or filled with false sincerity.

Of vast windbaggery and the absurd.
    It's just too much. I shout, "Spirit of Dowd!
How might I, humble drudge, in these sad times,
Defeat such turpitude with my poor rhymes?"

XVIII

"You think I've got the answer?" laughs the Muse.
    "I'm just a columnist. We like to think
We hold some clout, but really we just schmooze
    And write down third-hand gossip. Seas of ink
Are spilled for nothing. Yes, we point *j'accuse*;
    Occasionally we may kick up a stink
That might cause blushes; but that's very rare.
Most of the time we simply blow hot air.

XIX

"The president's an idiot, but folly
    Has been the stuff of politics forever.
He's not the first commander off his trolley
    And will not be the last. We might say 'Never
Again,' and yet we find ourselves, by golly,
    Once more with reprobates, pulling the lever
For someone who is chock-a-block with flaws
Yet whom we know will push our favorite cause.

XX

"This guy is big box-office. He's appalling,
    It's true, but equally compelling viewing.
He's always known that showing off's his calling
    Especially when he is scenery-chewing.

Turpitude. Depravity.

J'accuse. French for "I accuse," most famously used by Emile Zola in an 1898 letter, in
    which he accused the French government of anti-Semitism in the case of a Jewish
    military officer, Alfred Dreyfus, who was charged with treason.

What does he care if he's accused of balling
   Or doing what he just should *not* be doing?
It's part of his compulsion to convey a
Strong message that he'll always be a player.

XXI

"In your disparagement, where is the blame
   For Hillary, the Democrats, the press?
Obama was too cool; the blue team's game
   Was hoping trumpery would more or less
Hand Hillary the White House; or her name
   Was only what she needed to progress.
You never win because it is your turn,
That's what nomenklaturas never learn.

XXII

"I'm not denying race, misogyny,
   Or white fragility don't play a role;
The right dissembled, and 'identity'
   Works both ways. But, what's new? Sure, digging coal
And building walls aren't real policy,
   But class must count for something, and your goal
Of holding the Obama coalition
Failed in the face of working-class sedition.

XXIII

"You think that Sanders would have won the poll?
   A Jewish socialist who looks a mess?

Blue team's. Democratic states are traditionally depicted in blue, Republican in red.
Nomenklaturas. The name given to the political bureaucracy of the U.S.S.R.
Digging coal. The 2016 Republican candidate for president had promised to bring back coal jobs in depressed parts of West Virginia, Ohio, and Pennsylvania. The Obama coalition consisted of minorities, young people, and people with a college degree.
John Birch *manqué* **troll**. The John Birch Society was an anti-Communist, anti-Catholic, and anti-Semitic group set up in the 1950s. A troll is someone who posts comments on websites to stir up outrage, and *manqué* is French for someone who's failed to become what they'd hoped.

Each anti-Semite, John Birch *manqué* troll
    Would have attacked him, and with great success.
In days, they would have swallowed him up whole
    And fed his body to the right-wing press.
The young ones may have thought him hip and 'woke.'
But in the end he was the same old bloke.

XXIV

"So cut your blather, wise up, and get real.
    This man's a threat, yes; he must be opposed.
But your task is not simply to appeal
    To your own kind. You must be more hard-nosed,
And take down cant wherever, bring to heel
    The nonsense from the left-wing that's bulldozed
Its way through academe. Your form of group Id
Is just as dangerous and just as stupid.

XXV

"You're going to have to leave your comfort zone,
    And find out why your sort of liberal bias
Makes others squirm. You may employ high-flown
    Language to demonstrate why they are liars,
But that does not excuse your scornful tone,
    Preposterous conceits, and every pious
Assumption that each working-class Luddite,
Would, if he *listened* to you, see the light.

XXVI

"You know the story of the quid pro quo
    Between the Feds and Wall Street: heavyweights

"Woke". Socially conscious and aware of intersectional justice.
Luddite. An individual who resists technological change. The word comes from the textile
    workers who destroyed machinery in England in the early nineteenth century.
Quid pro quo. A reference to the government's bailout of banks and brokers following the
    financial crisis of 2007 and 2008.

In both blew right through our hard-earned dough
    And said, 'You pay: that's how it operates.'
If you'd been lent a pitchfork and flambeau
    You would have been the first to storm the gates.
Meanwhile, Joe Blow, Jane Doe—to their great grief—
Lost everything: car, cash, jobs, house, belief.

XXVII

"You said it: Uncle Sam and Liberty
    Were homeless. Look around you at the losses
To opioids, destitution, misery;
    The casual destruction of the bosses
Who ship their jobs abroad. Sure, you and me,
    We've got some money stowed away, our tosses
Are such that we can count on luck most days,
But if you have no cash, it's layaways

XXVIII

"And loan sharks, scams, and debt up to your ears.
    Do Chuck Schumer and others speak to this?
Do your soy latte–, smoothie-drinking peers
    Have any clue of what it's like to miss
Your payments and find yourself in arrears?
    Do you? In such a case, who cares for 'cis'
Or 'trans' or BLM? They're games to you
If your food doesn't last the whole day through.

Flambeau. A flaming torch.
Joe Blow, Jane Doe. Generic names for ordinary Americans.
To opioids. Deaths from overdoses from drug abuse in 2016 reached nearly 60,000, the majority from opioids such as heroin, fentanyl, and prescription medicine.
"Cis" or "trans". Cisgender and transgender are terms describing those whose gender matches the sex assigned to them when they were born, and those who don't, respectively. The sentiment reflects the belief among some that gender- and racial-identity politics inhibit social conservatives from voting for the Democratic Party.
BLM. Black Lives Matter is an organization that emerged following the killing of Trayvon Martin by George Zimmerman in Florida in 2013. The movement draws attention to the violence toward and killing of black people, including by law enforcement.

XXIX

"What you need is a story," she goes on.
    "You can't keep simply spouting derogation
Month after month. The Obama days are gone,
    And now we need a hero for the nation
To countermand this ass. An Amazon,
    Who'll be a legendary demonstration
Of what we could be. It may be pretend,
But at least we'll have fun before the end.

XXX

"Now, if you will excuse me, I'll be leaving.
    I really don't belong here with the dead:
I'm still alive (though looks may be deceiving).
    And while it's true I have a heavy tread
Like Orpheus, I'm not concerned with grieving
    The losses of a female figurehead.
The Clintons always have done very well
Each time they put their followers through hell."

XXXI

At that, she leaves (yes, in a puff of smoke),
    The Vices with her, while her scornful train
Throws me a glance, complaining what a joke
    It is I should have summoned her in vain,
Before they vanish in the gloom. I croak
    A brief farewell, then try to ascertain
Why she believed that it was mandatory:
To cast a hero who could lead a story.

Canto IV
April 2017

I

I'm cogitating on this, when appears
    Before me a familiar compound ghost.
The wry smile, weary mien beyond his years,
    And fierce disgust bear witness to a host
Of perfidies imposed upon his peers—
    Of murder, beatings—that would break the most
Resilient of souls. And yet his air
Betrays no trace of loathing or despair.

II

He turns to me: "No doubt, you've been advised
    To reach beyond the base to comprehend
What happened and why pollsters were surprised,
    And what message the voting might portend;
I'm sure you're pondering why the despised
    White working-class to whom you condescend
Would place their bets upon a slug and fop
Being the one who should come out on top."

Familiar compound ghost. Cf. T. S. Eliot's "Little Gidding," II: 42. Eliot, using tropes
found in Dante, is describing W. B. Yeats, who died in 1939. My ghost is at once James
Baldwin and a compound of voices of resistance to Dowd's notion that the Democrats
needed to reach out to the white working-class.

III

He says, "Always remember: from the start
 The 'patriots' made a determination
Of who would be considered 'us,' a part
 Of the rich fabric, who an aggravation.
No war, no act, no president, no art
 Can sound the depths of such repudiation,
Until together, honestly, we face
The scourge that is our legacy on race.

IV

"Obama isn't dumb, he knew his place
 In history could be a divagation;
That one black president would not erase
 The original evil of discrimination.
He realized we'd work to do to chase
 Away the fantasy that our foundation
Did not bake in injustice, bigotry,
And violence against people like me.

V

"How much this monster must hate 44:
 To be so pointedly and soundly mocked
By *him*—a witty, bright man, who could score
 Without assaulting women, and who rocked
With Jay Z and Beyoncé, and what's more
 Was not emasculated. He cock-blocked
White-male assumption and entitlement
That a black man could not be president.

Divagation. A digression.
Cock-blocked. A move designed to stop someone having sex.

VI

"You see it in his jutting chin, his stance,
    The swollen chest and extra lengthy tie;
His dread of being unmasked, the sidelong glance,
    The insecurity; his need to lie
And claim that *he's* the victim and enhance
    His image of himself as *the* good guy.
His confidence is obviously a trick;
A Jenga stack held by a single brick.

VII

"The man's a patsy, but even a sap
    Can dog whistle. The birth certificate;
The Central Park Five, the 'worst leader' crap—
    These tell white people what he means by 'great'
Is that he'll make black people doff their cap
    To massa once again, and what of late
We've gained will be rolled back. On this, he's sure:
Whiteness is normative, blackness impure.

VIII

"His posse of alt-right supremacists
    Shows noxious whiteness continues to fester;
Each washed-out, knock-kneed, sad sack that exists
    Believes George Washington is his ancestor;
Your pallid, inbred dragger-of-his-fists
    Insists that he's a paragon, the best a
Country like ours produces: but for proof
Who are they going to point to? Dylann Roof?

Jenga. A game in which players remove bricks from a stack piled high, with the aim of not bringing the whole thing crashing down.

Dog whistle. Phrases—particularly controversial ones—that convey a meaning beyond the ordinary sense of the phrase, much in the way a dog can hear sounds that humans can't.

Central Park Five. Five boys of color were imprisoned for raping a jogger in Central Park, New York City, in 1989. Their convictions were vacated in 2002, when another man confessed to the crime and DNA proved he did it. The current president has refused to recant his belief (which he stated at the time) that the boys were guilty.

IX

"Now, liberals like you want to be cleared
    Of guilt by melanin association.
But name a time when black men were not smeared
    By similar slurs: sexual predation,
Assault, rebellion? Or black men feared
    White women's words against them? Friend, this nation
Is steeped in hate and dread that's so extensive,
That your weak 'It's not me!' is plain offensive.

X

"That's why I'm tired of being told to wait
    For white America to 'get it.' No,
It's said, it's not their fault that what was great
    To them leaves out Friedan, Vietnam, Jim Crow,
And whom you couldn't love or even date
    Without some buzz-cut clown or GI Joe
Beating the shit out of you every day,
Joined by his righteous pals, the KKK.

XI

"It's hard to face such privilege: to admit
    That poor and sick and jobless though you are,
You don't, won't ever, think that you don't fit;
    That your translucent pelt bears you so far
Beyond your brother's tanned hide. To submit
    To such a truth would throw off your North Star.
For Liberty's and Uncle Sam's pale skins
Absolve you of a multitude of sins.

Vietnam. The Vietnam War (1955–1975) led to the deaths of hundreds of thousands of Vietnamese and 58,000 American soldiers.

Jim Crow. The popular name given to the segregationist and racist policies of the American South from the end of Reconstruction to the Civil Rights Act of 1965.

GI Joe. The generic name for an American soldier.

KKK. The Ku Klux Klan, a racist and anti-Semitic terrorist organization.

XII

"Ironically, we black folks want to cleave
　　To what this nation promises to all.
In spite of crackers telling us to 'Leave!
　　Go back to Africa' each day, we fall
For jingoistic humbug, sit and weave
　　The beautiful illusion that the small
Improvements in our lives will one day lead
To a time when no more black children will bleed."

XIII

He stops and draws upon his cigarette.
　　"Well, there it is. 'My country, 'tis of thee.'"
He looks me up and down. "Now, don't forget,"
　　He adds, "That words can soothe too easily
The soul of heartache. And it's a good bet
　　That's what you're hoping for; that you will see
Safe passage through the muck. But it's much harder
To stoke your rage and reignite your ardor.

XIV

"Write what you will, you'll never be Du Bois.
　　You cannot claim to 'sing America.'
Red, white, or blue—your color is a choice
　　Where we are always black." He paused. "We are
Always the other. So, you use your voice
　　In any way you wish, take it as far
As you can go. I wish you luck, you'll need it:
A middling gift with only pique to feed it."

Cracker. Black American slang for a white person.
"My country 'tis of thee". The first line of "America," a patriotic song composed by
　　Samuel Francis Smith in 1831.
"Sing America". Part of the first line of African-American poet Langston Hughes' "I,
　　Too," which was itself a reflection on Walt Whitman's "I Hear America Singing."

XV

At that, he disappears into the haze.
    I breathe out and reflect. It seems my fate
Is not to wreathe my head with laurel bays
    But to be shown by writers, live and late,
The insufficiency of my poor lays
    In apprehending the affairs of state.
Dejected, I trudge slowly to the exit,
When from the mist a Frenchman cries out, "*Sex* it."

XVI

I raise my head and, lo, in some decay,
    In front of me is *the* Marquis de Sade.
Chuckling and gibbering, *déshabillé*,
    Scratching his flaking scalp, clearly half-mad,
He bows extravagantly: "*Bonne soirée*
    To him, the downer! Sir, you're feeling bad
About your prospects as a satirist.
Might I, a humble hedonist, assist?"

XVII

I nod. What, really, do I have to lose?
    "Your trouble, m'sieur, is that you're too polite.
Even Ms. Dowd—her talent's to amuse,
    Not scandalize; the other's to be right.
But *real* satire doesn't pick and choose
    Whom to be friends with and with whom to fight.
The point is not to be mellow and pensive;
But to be universally offensive.

Laurel bays. In Roman times, laurel wreaths were awarded for poetic excellence.
Lays. A poetic word for poetic songs. Often spelled *lais*.
Marquis de Sade. The political and social satirist (1740–1814) was known for his obscene
    works (which satirize politics and clericalism), including *The 120 Days of Sodom*.
Déshabillé. French for "scantily dressed."
Bonne soirée. French for "good night."

XVIII

"What better way than sex to spill the bedpan
    And pour forth streams of effluence and stink;
You may ejaculate or stick to deadpan,
    Evoke a burlesque babe or slim-hipped twink,
But whether you give or like getting head, man,
    Dig 'in your face' or more 'nudge, nudge, wink wink,'
Sex breaks down every barrier and taboo,
Because whom you shaft will in turn shaft you.

XIX

"The priest caught pants-down with his catamite,
    The statesman rifling through his mistress' drawers;
The moralist found naked at dawn's light
    Bound by a dominatrix on all fours;
The socialite whose sateless appetite
    For rough trade opens legs, hearts, and class doors:
These illustrate desire is unrestrained,
However we might wish it be contained.

XX

"The judges thrashed by minxes in their nighties,
    The wise guys felled by languorous brunettes,
The cops fellated in their tighty-whities,
    The Dixiecrats impaled by black coquettes,
The honeytraps who snare the high-and-mighties,

Twink. Gay slang for a slender homosexual of boyish appearance.
"Nudge, nudge, wink, wink". The most famous tagline from a sketch by the British comedy sextet Monty Python, in which Eric Idle plays a customer annoying the straight-laced Terry Jones in a pub, using innuendo to comic effect.
Catamite. A pre-pubescent boy used for the purposes of sex.
Rough trade. British slang for working-class male sex workers.
Minx. Slang for a sexy woman.
Tighty-whities. Snug white briefs for men.
Dixiecrats. Southern Democrats of the Jim Crow era, who supported racial segregation.
Honeytrap. A woman employed by others to seduce a man for the purposes of blackmail.

The teens on the back seats of their Corvettes:
These testify to the lordly misrule
That renders sex the satirist's best tool.

XXI

"The MILF who finds the plumber's snake most handy,
    The blonde who dives into a mogul's pocket;
The lingam that licks each yogini's candy,
    The tux who shoots the deb off like a rocket;
The cad whose mick slips in the virgin's shandy:—
    As every plug fits snugly in its socket
So sex supplies the necessary juice
That froths the foam of fountains of abuse.

XXII

"The Mennonite who trolls for ladyboys,
    The imam who courts his hermaphrodite,
The Hasidim cruising the streets for goys,
    The monk who stains his habit every night,
The nun whose bedside table's full of toys,
    Renunciates whom lust comes back to bite
Reveal a strain of sex that's anti-clerical
But cannot be dismissed as just chimerical.

MILF. Acronym taken from the popular movie *American Pie* (1999) to describe a "mother I'd like to fuck."
Lingam. The Hindu symbol for the archetypal penis, or source of male energy.
Mick. A "micky finn" or drug that renders the victim unconscious. Here it's also used as another word for penis.
Shandy. A mixture of lemonade and beer. Here it's used as a synonym for vagina.
Mennonite. A particularly pious and puritanical protestant sect.
Ladyboys. Transsexual Asian men who identify as women.
Chimerical. An illusion. This stems from the chimera, a hybrid beast of Greek mythology composed of different animals' body parts.

XXIII

"So, my advice is stop being so pious
    About what's wrong. Ignore the culturati;
When has there ever been a time when bias
    For one's own blood, land, ethnic group, or party
Did not rule hearts? The politicians ply us
    With nostrums that lead us to think we're smart, we
Compound our vanities with the fixation
That history bends to amelioration.

XXIV

"But hate and prejudice are unremitting,
    In every decade thoughtlessness renewed.
Elites gain pleasure regularly shitting
    Upon the schmucks who itch to be subdued.
They let the shysters take their power, pitting
    Themselves against their fellows to collude
With hucksters whose main message (finely honed)
Is, 'I'll make sure the other guy is boned.'

XXV

"So, damn each conscientious Pharisee
    Who never votes because 'it's just a sham';
The mouth-breather who says, 'He speaks for me,'
    When douche-y hacks upchuck their aural spam;
The selfish tightwad who only feels free
    To get involved when *he* is in a jam:
These morons with their regular apostasies—
Are nothing but the ass-wipes of democracies.

Boned. British slang for sexual intercourse.
Pharisee. A religious hypocrite.
Douche-y. Like an idiot: a disparaging term coined from a feminine hygiene product.

44

XXVI

"Through their inertia or their votes they got
　　What they deserved: a venal, oily fake,
As disengaged and ignorant as the lot
　　Of them; a lazy, good-for-nothing rake
Who aims to yank the handle of each slot
　　Machine of government to cash in, make
A ton more money on cable TV,
And once again bankrupt the bourgeoisie.

XXVII

"Your task, then, is to let it all hang out.
　　Imagine those two Russian hookers humping
Above his orange corpulence; the lout
　　(Wearing a shower cap) enjoys them dumping
Their piss into his navel; but the sprout
　　That is his dick he can't prevent from slumping
Each time a golden drop lands with a splat,
In panic that this might be *kompromat*.

XXVIII

"We know the pussy-grabber craves patootie.
　　He longs to let his grubby fingers roam.
Think of his sweaty crevices, the fruity
　　Pong of his cheap cologne. When he gets home

Two Russian hookers. According to a report produced by British spy Christopher Steele, in 2013, during the Miss World pageant in Moscow, the 2016 Republican candidate hired two prostitutes to urinate on a hotel bed that he believed Barack and Michelle Obama had slept in.

Kompromat. A Russian word for compromising information or material.

Pussy-grabber. The name given to the 2016 Republican presidential candidate following the release of a 2005 audiotape from the TV show *Access Hollywood*, in which the former told host Billy Bush that he, the candidate, "grabbed" women "by the pussy."

Patootie. American slang for a pretty woman.

And boasts to gamesmen playing 'Call of Booty,'
　　Imagine women smearing cleansing foam
Within each orifice the mountebank
　　Has pawed, or into which his damp lips sank."

XXIX

The old lech stops and grins. "Feel better now?"
　　He leers. "The artist's role is overrated:
In Hades no one ever gives a cow
　　At what you wrote. So much of it is dated
And every name forgotten, anyhow.
　　Whether you're scandalous or understated
Most will ignore your thoughts in all respects
But one—and that is when you speak of sex."

XXX

He waves me off and, fortified, I rise
　　Until the surface of the earth I meet.
Before me spring has lightened up the skies
　　The flowers bloom and songbirds dart and tweet.
My time in hell has given me supplies
　　With which to tune my wit and scrub my feet.
My task is clear: without doubt or revision,
To stand and fight in total opposition.

'Call of Booty'. A play on the popular video game "Call of Duty,"—*booty* being slang for
　　the buttocks, especially of the female.
Mountebank. A showy swindler.
A cow. To become angry or upset. A paraphrase of "Don't have a cow," a phrase popular-
　　ized by the character Bart on the long-running TV cartoon show, *The Simpsons*.

Canto V

May 2017

Prelude

Let fly the flags; resistance songs upraise;
    As one, chant slogans and hope reignite:
For we have made it through a hundred days.

We were convinced that he would set ablaze
    The Constitution, and let the alt-right
Fly their false flags as long as he got praise

Pursuing strongman tactics and mores.
    We thought the nation would end overnight,
But we have made it through a hundred days.

The president continually displays
    His rank incompetence. But now in sight
Are warning flags voters will reappraise

What's tolerable. Will he let malaise
    Entomb us, or conjure distress and fright
To terrorize the next one hundred days?

Prelude. A villanelle. Unlike conventional villanelles, the first line, which is usually repeated as the last line of alternate stanzas, plays with the various cognate and homophonic forms of the word *praise*.

Who knows? It never ceases to amaze
    How much confusion, contumely, and spite
His flagging, on-the-fly rule spits up: rays

Of light we see, but in too many ways,
It's clear the worst is yet to come: so, fight!
Let fly the flags; resistance songs upraise;
That we may live another hundred days.

* * *

I

Now I've returned from Hades, I am bound
    To ponder how to prosecute my story.
My muse has told me that another round
    Of *o me miserum* or (short of glory)
Cheap shots and gripe will only make me sound
    A whining malcontent. Much better for me
And readers, she's said, to conjure a fighter
Who'll do the necessary to the blighter.

II

Perhaps she wants a hunk who's lithe and lusty,
    To fight against our leader's callous vanity.
He's somewhat dim perhaps, but brave and trusty.
    His steadfastness will shame the cruel inanity,
And what is piecemeal, shambolic, or crusty
    About the administration. His humanity
Will shine through in his dash and derring-do
And strike a marked contrast with You Know Who.

Contumely. Spite.
O me miserum. A Latin tag meaning, "O wretched me."

III

When asked to serve, he'll lift the nearest blade
    And rush to fight without much preparation.
He'll down the enemy and won't be stayed
    Though one might wish for a sign of mentation.
And while as subtle as a hand-grenade
    Our hero will provide some compensation
In that before he's righted every wrong,
He'll trill a leitmotifed chromatic song.

IV

C'est vrai, the danger with the martial sort
    Is that he can't take domesticity.
Once war is over, he returns to port;
    And after he's kissed his Penelope,
And she's told him to cut the hedge and sort
    His man-cave out and clean the lavatory,
He starts to think it would be quite a wheeze
To sail through the Pillars of Hercules

V

And westward to the sunset. I prefer,
    Someone who's blessed with brains and guile and cunning,
Who'll toss each pencil-pusher and poseur
    A withering bon mot to send them running;
Whose wit will cut to ribbons each frotteur
    Who rubs him the wrong way artlessly punning,
And rend their orifices raw and tender.
No, let's leave him alone, and change the gender.

Leitmotifed chromatic song. A *leitmotif* is a musical phrase that signifies a character or mood. It was used widely by German composer Richard Wagner, whose character Siegfried in the *Ring* cycle of operas is referenced here.

Penelope. In some versions of the story, Odysseus tires of domesticity in Ithaca, and sets sail westwards beyond the Pillars of Hercules, which is what the Ancients called the Straits of Gibraltar. I am recalling Alfred, Lord Tennyson's poem "Ulysses."

Frotteur. A man who receives sexual gratification by rubbing his penis against another person's clothing.

VI

Let us dream up an awesome warrior queen
    Who'll grapple with the groper and his clan;
With gimlet eye and steady gaze she'll clean
    The clocks of every spineless congressman
Who tells her that gals like her should be seen
    And not heard. While reciting Thich Nhat Hanh,
She'll grip his scrotum in an iron fist
And should he not be truly mindful, twist.

VII

Or someone understated, shy, petite,
    Yet five foot two of compact dynamite.
She gets her nous and savvy from the street,
    And knows when to give way and when to fight.
A Daoist ninja warrior, who's quite sweet
    Unless you cross her, then this mighty sprite
Will unleash merry hell upon your cheeks
Until you can't park your sore tush for weeks.

VIII

I get that Byron was being sarcastic
    When he implied heroes were two a penny.
Partly, of course, since (far from periphrastic)
    He could halloo his own achievements when he
Rained down his scorn, either wry or bombastic.
    I don't possess half of his talents; any
New Britomart that I cause to appear
Will likely flop before she shakes her spear.

Nous. Intelligence.
Tush. Slang for buttocks.
Periphrastic. Circumlocutory.

IX

It's possible that for the Kali Yuga
    The goddess, skull-bedecked, would suit, or Shiva;
Or someone *au courant* like Freddy Krueger
    Could hand out his sharp nightmares; and "throng-cleaver"
That Gimli wields or Christoph Waltz's luger
    Might do the trick. Or (more *Leave It to Beaver*
And much less bloody) we could in a pinch
Call Clarence Darrow or Atticus Finch.

X

The movies are replete with Marvel Comics
    Heroes and villains, mutants and X-men.
I'm tired of such unhappy souls: where's Tom Mix
    To thunder to the rescue, or John Glenn
To once more thrill us with his astronomics?
    Wolf Man, Catwoman, Amber, Kylo Ren
Might move some merchandise: but times are drastic—
Since real life is ten times more phantastic.

XI

In sum, it's hard to locate a game-changer
    Since any character is trumped by fact.
You think each day cannot get any stranger,
    Yet whether through crime, misdeed, or compact,
Another scandal bursts, another danger
    To the world order: set up to distract
From some grand ruse or mere incompetence?
And do we even know the difference?

Kali Yuga. Within the Hindu cosmic timescale, the Kali Yuga is the most recent and most depraved of current ages. Kali is the Hindu goddess of destruction.
Shiva. The Hindu god of creation and destruction.
Leave It to Beaver. The 1950s and 1960s American TV show is synonymous with wholesome, family-values entertainment.

XII

What fresh hell can this be? we gasp and sigh.
　　Let's summarize what we have learned to date.
In Spring last year, Justice, the F.B.I.,
　　And others partnered to investigate
Attempts by Russian hackers to deny
　　A free and fair election; fabricate
Fake news; and, by release of Dems' emails,
Avert notice from G.O.P. travails.

XIII

The six-agency group aspires to find
　　Who paid the hackers. Meanwhile, House and Senate
Intelligence committees are assigned
　　To find out just who was behind it, when it
Occurred, and what effect it had. The mind
　　Would need the wisdom of a Daniel Dennett
To calculate every ramification
Of each conjecturable machination.

XIV

Why was the House Intel Committee chair
　　Meeting with staffers in the dead of night?
What info did he get and did he share
　　And on what planet would he think this right?
What does Mike Flynn know? Will we find out where
　　Both Manafort and Page fit in? Will light
Be shed on Russia's role in the campaign
Or will dissimulation win again?

What fresh hell can this be? A quote attributed to American humorist Dorothy Parker.
G.O.P. The "Grand Old Party," another name for the Republican Party.
House Intel Committee Chair. Republican Devin Nunes was accused of passing informa-
　　tion about the Congressional investigation into Russia's hacking of the U.S. elections to
　　the White House. He has denied any wrongdoing.

XV

How should we comprehend each hour's claims?
    Russia was once the flavor of the day,
But now is wrong and China right; war-games
    For World War III with the D.P.R.K.
Go on apace; each tidy set of aims
    In foreign policy in every way
Is tossed aside. Existence is at stake:
Yet missiles are launched over chocolate cake.

XVI

Meanwhile, we pray that Jared and Ivanka
    Kindly employ their finely tailored gloss
And slick PR skills as a kind of a Sanka
    To water down their caffeinated boss.
But even they can't hide the fact this wanker
    Is without scruple, couldn't give a toss
About a single thing but saving face
With those he says he represents: his base.

XVII

Bizarre it is, like Midas in reverse,
    That what he touches turns from "gold" to crap.
For Billy Bush was thriving, then the curse
    Of his off-camera remarks' mishap
Saw him thrown off his primetime show, and worse,
    The man who egged him on avoids the rap
To ride his "locker-room" identity
To an unconscionable victory.

D.P.R.K. North Korea: the Democratic People's Republic of Korea.

Chocolate cake. When Chinese Premier Xi Jinping met with 45 at the latter's residence in Mar-a-Lago, Florida in April, the former was astonished when the latter launched 59 missiles against an airbase in Syria while chocolate cake was being served. The bombing followed media reports of a chemical weapons attack by the Syrian government on a rebel-held stronghold.

XVIII

And Bill O'Reilly, old-white-people bait,
    And fan because he boosts his Nielsen rating,
Is felt up by the little hands of fate.
    Women talk of his calls while masturbating,
Unwanted propositions for a date,
    And, though Bill's forced to go (true, with a grating
Financial deal), his erstwhile guest can blabber
(Unpunished) how he is a pussy-grabber.

XIX

Now Roger Ailes, Steve Bannon, and Paul Ryan
    Have had their wings clipped (Flynn might go to jail).
Chaffetz is done, Nunes is toast, and Lyin'
    Ted has not been heard from. And I would quail
If I were Roger Stone. Only a scion
    It seems is safe from being doomed to fail.
Advice to pols: think of ways not to show
If you're invited to Mar-a-Lago.

XX

The irony is that he's not the lone
    Villainous fool or showy would-be king,
Whose arrogant, half-macho half-cornpone
    Belief is *l'etat c'est moi* posturing—

"Locker-room". When the *Access Hollywood* tape aired in October 2016 (see "Bush, Billy"), the Republican presidential nominee defended his comments about assaulting women as only "locker-room talk."

Nielsen rating. The means by which it's determined how popular a TV show is, and therefore how much advertising money it can command.

Little hands of fate. During the 2016 campaign for the nomination for president, the eventual G.O.P. nominee was ridiculed by other candidates for his small hands, as a symbol of his diminished manhood. The nominee protested this characterization of his penis during a televised debate.

Lyin' Ted. Ted Cruz.

Mar-a-Lago. The private club to which 45 retreated during 2017. He owns it.

L'etat c'est moi. "I am the state." Saying attributed to Louis XIV of France (1638–1715).

They want to think they're like Don Corleone:
    Dispensing grace with a kiss of the ring.
And (if you're President Rody Duterte)
    Ensuring that drug dealers don't reach thirty.

XXI

In Turkey, Recep Tayyip Erdoğan
    Has commandeered the state and now can reign
Until he's seventy-five. And, deadly spawn,
    Young Chairman Kim has decades left of pain
To inflict on his poor country. Woe upon,
    Poor Egypt, Venezuela, and the bane
Of those who hope for peace—Putin-Assad:
That murderous hybrid of what is bad.

XXII

Jeb Bush called him the "chaos candidate."
    Some pundits say it could prove advantageous
For him whose moves one can't anticipate
    To challenge sacred cows; the more outrageous
The move, the crazier that it might rate,
    The more a realignment that this magus
May conjure: well, I'm not sure what they're drinking,
But this is nothing more than wishful thinking.

Egypt. Since taking power in 2014, Egyptian president Abdel Fattah el-Sisi has repressed dissent, jailed the opposition, and consolidated power.

Venezuela. In the summer of 2017, President Nicolás Maduro abrogated political power from the other democratic bodies as a means of remaining in office.

Putin-Assad. Vladimir Putin's supplying of military and financial assistance is widely credited for the turnaround in the Syrian government's military and political fortunes. In 2017, the six-year-long civil war in Syria saw the retreat of ISIS, the destruction of forces opposed to President Bashar al-Assad, and further destabilization of the region.

Jeb Bush. On December 15, 2015. He prophesied he'd also be a "chaos president."

Pundits say. Conservative pundit David Brooks was one of them.

XXIII

Chaos by definition's uncontrolled;
    It's always prettier before it starts.
Strategic brinkmanship to break the mold
    Is well and good, but sometimes finer arts
Of statecraft, knowing when it's good to fold,
    Are needed to resolve the harder parts.
Khrushchev and Kennedy in sixty-two
Saw Armageddon if they saw it through.

XXIV

We *assume* that Kim Jong-un's not really crazy
    But ups the ante to suppress dissent.
We *assume* the president won't ape Scorsese
    And that he'll cool the jaw-jaw to prevent
War breaking out. For now, Goldwater's daisy
    Remains unplucked, but merely to foment
A crisis to prove that you can draw faster
Will, in this case, lead only to disaster.

XXV

Rex Tillerson tells us that regime change
    Is not the aim, just a nuke-free Korea;
The generals around him will arrange
    A peaceful climbdown—there's no need to fear
That he'll go off half-cocked. Is it not strange
    That in this escapade it is not clear
Just who we mean? For what we say of Kim
Could just as readily apply to him.

Jaw-jaw. The motto "jaw, jaw is better than war, war," is usually attributed to Winston Churchill, but was actually said by another British prime minister, Harold Macmillan.

Goldwater's daisy. In 1964, the Democratic Party developed a TV advertisement against Barry Goldwater (1909–1998), Republican nominee for president. It depicted a girl plucking a daisy during the countdown to a nuclear explosion. The ad was never aired but was widely talked about.

XXVI

Is it not wacky that it's Xi Jinping
    To whom we turn to calm the situation?
That moderation might come from Beijing
    Cannot but make my head twirl, for this nation
(Once this man's *bête noire*) now commands the ring,
    Can get any sort of accommodation
On Taiwan, Spratly Islands' reefs, Tibet,
That it wants from its new best friend and pet.

XXVII

Meanwhile, health care repeal's snagged again,
    The vaunted tax plan's but a single sheet;
The economy hums on; we wait in vain
    For the great infrastructure bill; Main Street
Continues to endure the opioid pain;
    The Muslim ban's tied up in court; the seat
Of government is stalled while national treasures
Are compromised for the extractors' pleasures.

XXVIII

So we return to letting plutocrats
    And plunderers despoil, deface, and spill.
And while this fragile planet warms, fat cats
    And their investors take no care, nor will

Taiwan. The People's Republic of China has long maintained a "One China" policy toward this island—a policy 45, early in his administration, questioned before reversing himself.

Spratly Islands. Contested islands in the South China Sea that China is currently developing and expanding as a staging post for its naval and air forces.

Tibet. China invaded Tibet in 1949 and has ruled it ever since.

Muslim ban. In February, 45 attempted to pass a ban against individuals entering from seven Muslim-majority countries, only to be stayed by court orders. The stay was partially lifted by the Supreme Court, pending a full judgment on the ban, which was decided in the 45's favor in December.

The government hold them to account: for stats
    And warnings won't stop them firing the grill.
So, yes, *plus ça change, plus c'est la même chose*;
But why should I accept such status quos?

XXIX

I pen this just before the climate rally
    Will gather in D.C. to call for action—
This quarter century marks a sad tally
    Of thwarted goals, missed targets, lack of traction
Among the people. We still shilly shally
    Or (worse) give time and credence to a fraction
That claims that scientists exaggerate
The effect of climate change and we should wait.

XXX

For what? Until Miami's in the ocean,
    The permafrost has thawed, poles open seas?
When Byron wrote his poetry, the notion
    That we might end life in four centuries
Would have been risible, but now in motion
    Is warming of four, even six, degrees,
Not seen on Earth for millions of years.
How is not this the sum of our fears?

XXXI

How is not this the focus of this era?
    Why aren't we doing now what must be done
To end the use of fossil fuels; bring nearer
    New skills and policies so more than one

Plus ça change. French: "The more things change, the more they remain the same."
Climate rally. The People's Climate March occurred on April 29, 2017.

Or two of us survive? What could be clearer
 Than this grim task? Yet what son of a gun
Is leading us into the deepest hole
But he who thinks the answer is "More coal!"?

Canto VI

June 2017

I

June is upon us, and we're six months in.
　　Each day brings more alarm and conflagration.
Each month I find it harder to begin
　　My task without dread and exasperation.
Yet, *pace* Dowd, De Sade, and James Baldwin,
　　A blanket character assassination
Does not come easily to me. And why?
Because we're both born under Gemini.

II

Now I know what you're thinking: that it's crazy
　　To think astrology can hold the key
To understanding how he ticks—a lazy,
　　Reductive stand-in for psychiatry
That lacks a scientific structure for the ways he
　　Determines his reality to be.
But my aim is not psychotherapeutic,
But mythopoetic and hermeneutic.

Pace. Latin for "in peace," and meaning, "In deference to, but in disagreement, with."
Mythopoetic. Relating to, or the act of, creating myths.
Hermeneutic. Relating to, of the act of, interpretation.

III

We Geminis are ruled by Mercury,
    Quicksilver god of messages and trade.
A puckish trickster, always moving, he
    Can talk his way out of an escapade,
Employ seduction to the nth degree,
    And wave his hands like weapons to persuade
You into thinking that it would be great
To hand him moola or go on a date.

IV

Unfettered by the need to say what's true,
    Ungrounded by responsibility,
We Geminis love searching for what's new—
    New friends, new baubles, new places to be
Where all the action is. However, through
    Legerdemain or glib aside, we flee
When we feel that we are constrained or bored,
Or even worse, belittled or ignored.

V

Mere light and air, we have no shadow side:
    Commercial skill is also greed for money.
We can sell anything, and we're both snide
    And blithe; we're quick, we're cruel, *and* we're funny.
God of transitions, Mercury can slide
    From one mood to the next: one moment sunny,
The next a pouting child. We're in the know,
But, if you ask "about what?" we must go!

Quicksilver. Mercurial.
Puckish. Like the character of Puck in *A Midsummer Night's Dream*: mischievous, playful, impish.
Moola. Slang for money.
Legerdemain. Sleight of hand.

VI

Like Dug the cartoon dog in *Up!* we're swayed
    By any passing fad or observation.
(*Squirrel!*) We are good-naturedly waylaid
    By surface shininess, improvisation,
And gossip. Anything that is too staid
    Or needs a molecule of concentration
Can make us want to run or raise our guard:
We do not like what's complex or what's hard.

VII

In spite of attributes that are alarming
    It's hard for us always to be malicious.
We're much more comfortable being charming.
    We don't like direct conflict; we're ambitious,
First, to seal the deal by disarming,
    And, second, make the buyer like us. Vicious
Retorts and personal attacks come later,
Should we fail to wow as an instigator.

VIII

Therefore, my (tepid) rancor might be due
    To that I see myself in him. How much
We crave the spotlight . . . only for the view:
    Pretending that we have the common touch,
We fret that we'll be judged a parvenu
    And not up to the task. So, as a crutch
We bluster that *of course* we have a plan, sir!
(As long as we can make it through the stanza.)

Parvenu. An arriviste or social upstart.

IX

That said, I'd like to hope I'd practice caution,
 Restrain myself from speaking off the cuff.
I'd want my staff to keep things in proportion
 And say when I've done or not done enough.
I think I'd know to delegate, for sure shun
 Contempt and defamation, take the rough
And smooth as equal parts of holding power,
And not measure achievement by the hour.

X

I trust I'd want to know the truth from lies,
 And that I'd not be frightened of dissent.
I hope I'd face my faults and not disguise
 The danger facing any president
Of only seeking good news or the highs
 And pomp of office. I would not prevent
A range of views from being aired before me,
And I would not ask people to adore me.

XI

I'll never be the Commander in Chief
 And so can tell myself I'd have a heart
And would behave. It comes as some relief
 That Taurus is ascendant in my chart,
Which gives me discipline. But that bold thief,
 Light-fingered Hermes, can outdo, outsmart
Those who would tie him down. And don't expect
Him to be cool, serene, or circumspect.

XII

The restlessness of Mercury's a blessing:
    If ousted, he will find someone to blame
And move on to the next thing. No point stressing
    Disgrace to Hermes, for he has no shame.
In fact, he might already (I am guessing)
    Be formulating a sly plot to game
Washington, D.C., so he can exact
The maximal revenge for being sacked.

XIII

All things considered, I have thus concluded
    It's not a superhero that we need.
To pine for an immortal is deluded,
    A vanity despair and weakness feed;
A wish the idle and the hope-denuded
    Use to avoid the worry they'll succeed
If they rose up and fought for recognition:
The comfort of unnoticed opposition.

XIV

The paradox is that this fake and fraud
    Pretends to speak the "truth" of discontent.
Those who believe they've been ignored applaud
    Someone they wanted to blow up consent
And take their country back. This sham and bawd,
    Who only cares about himself, was meant
To be the people's tribune and to fight
So they'd receive what they thought theirs by right.

XV

O double treachery! The boob and pill
    Is too incompetent for his agenda:
He has no understanding of the Hill
    And each day he blurts out random addenda,
Errors, tirades, redactions that will kill
    The legislation. Each speech in the blender
Makes an already hard job even tougher,
As well as those who voted for him suffer.

XVI

The second insult: what he's getting done
    Does *nothing* for his base. The health-care plan
That passed the House (no matter how it's spun)
    Will hurt the poor and old. Yet, this conman
Told folks his scheme would be the best, bar none:
    For whom?'s the question. How a person can
So wantonly mislead those who believed
Is shocking even to me, the undeceived.

XVII

The Muslim ban won't stop one terrorist;
    The tax cuts will not help the middle-class.
The budget ends the programs that assist
    The hard-hit regions, jobless, and the mass
Of people in the red states, who have kissed
    Their welfare net goodbye. A coup de grâce
Will surely come when, sometime in the fall,
They realize he will not build the Wall.

XVIII

Thus, more supporters will become addicted,
    And, due to Sessions, spend more time in jail.
The infrastructure bill, which was depicted
    As quasi-multi-partisan, will fail
Because he doesn't care for the afflicted
    Who need jobs, hope, and luck. So he will bail
On the few promises he's not discarded
To fantasize that he's still well-regarded.

XIX

We do not need a Storm or Wolverine:
    What we demand is one Republican
Or ten to say, "He can no more demean
    The office of the president. This man
Is not up to the task, and the obscene
    Series of follies that define the span
Of his administration must be ended.
He can no longer by us be defended."

XX

I don't expect McConnell, Cornyn, Cruz,
    Paul Ryan, and other G.O.P. hacks
To stand up and be counted. They refuse
    To get a spine or stiffen their bent backs.
As long as they think they have more to lose
    By ditching him, they'll not bring down the ax.
These profiles of gutless hypocrisy
Won't move until it's risk- and conscience-free.

XXI

But I assume you're not like them, Ben Sasse.
    I hear they walk tall in Plainview, Nebraska.
I like to think you're in a different class
    From every other cheap-jack. It's a task a
Straightshooter from the heartland could amass
    Thanks of a grateful nation for: unmask a
Disreputable charlatan, and teach him
A lesson he won't soon forget. Impeach him!

XXII

What hope that Lindsey Graham, John McCain,
    And Pat Toomey will proclaim, "That's enough!"?
What more is needed, Sue Collins of Maine,
    To show that you are made of sterner stuff?
Lisa Murkowski surely can't maintain
    Her silence. And what happened to the bluff
Bob Corker or John Thune of South Dakota?
I can't believe you don't care one iota.

XXIII

Leaving aside each crime and misdemeanor,
    Endangering the sources and intel;
Ignoring that he makes Anthony Weiner
    Look cherubic; and avoiding, as well,
How he and his clan couldn't be obscener
    In their extravagances, what the hell
Do you believe should be the repercussions
Of being so damn cozy with the Russians?

XXIV

But who is this who's coming to the rescue?
    A gray-haired white dude, name of Robert Mueller.
The F.B.I. guy will weed out the fescue
    And flush the bushes to find if our ruler
Is innocent, a Nicolae Ceauşescu,
    Or simply just a grown-up Ferris Bueller
Who can't hack working. With deliberation,
We hope Bob saves us from disintegration.

XXV

I trust Mueller will take his time (a friend),
    For Mercury hates pressure. He's already
Tweeting his outrage, umbrage that won't end
    Even outside the White House. But the heady
Mixture of revelations might impend
    His losing his ascendancy. Instead, he
Will prefer to prop up his precious brand
Rather than carry on taking a stand.

XXVI

At that point, he'll claim the system's corrupt,
    That Washington was always out to get him.
He'll bellyache the politicians sucked
    And that he hated everyone who met him.
He'll state without his leadership we're fucked
    And we'll be sorry that we have upset him.
Licking his wounds, he'll go back to his Tower
Like Sauron, and wait to restore his power.

Fescue. A particularly tenacious ornamental grass.

XXVII

I hope they throw the book at him, I do.
    I hope they toss his helmet, clip his heels,
And force him to confess and grovel, too.
    I hope they probe his actions till he squeals
So he can know what he has put us through,
    And recognize what each one of us feels.
I hope that those who voted for him see
How bad he was, is, and will always be.

XXVIII

Yet, knowing him and us, he'll find a way
    To avoid more than a mild slap on the wrist.
For he's America—Live for the day!
    Give him another chance! Let's co-exist!—
Or, at the least, the rich, white man's cachet
    Allows him to walk off into the mist
With millions in his termination packet
That lets him finance yet another racket.

XXIX

So Hermes laughs again—the kid takes flight:
    Spreading his rumors, throwing cash around,
And joining A and B with C. Delight
    Aerates his freedom, animates each bound.
Wired each day and sleepless through the night,
    He makes sure his feet never touch the ground:
The Peter Pan of endless broken vows,
The boy who stole Apollo's sacred cows.

XXX

More seriously, what shall we conclude
    About these disunited states we live in:
That we allowed someone plainly unglued
    To be the leader? Will we be forgiven
By those who follow us and whom we've screwed?
    To whom will our souls turn to be shriven
When we're confronted in the coming years
With blood and sweat and toil and seas of tears?

Canto VII
July 2017

I

He rises up before you every day
    (Or so it seems): the blotchy, fleshy face;
The blank-eyed stare; the hair in disarray
    Or greased back. From his purple nose, you trace
The booze or drugs, the broken veins that splay
    Across the sallow skin. And to displace
His weak chin, *the* token of pedigree:
The contoured, gray-flecked, middle-aged goatee.

II

Each mugshot shows a flattened vacancy,
    Ambitions bleached, and half-held vows ignored,
A faint hint of respectability
    Amid the self-inflicted wreckage. Bored
Eyes narrow in contempt or glint with glee
    At what he takes as some kind of reward:
If it required *this* as an audition,
Then it was worth the price of ammunition.

III

No doubt a man who liked the quiet life,
    Who loved his guns, his Harley, and a beer.
But recently, he'd found out that his wife
    Was seeing Pablo from accounts. The fear
Of cuckoldry had cut him like a knife.
    That Friday, he'd loaded his hunting gear
And brought down both with his AR-15:
His self-respect ensured his shots were clean.

IV

He didn't go to church much, but he knew
    Some Bible stuff, and he had read online
About Islam. "I've got my eye on you,"
    He told Virat in sales. "One move, you're mine."
Virat just smiled, but two weeks later grew
    Concerned enough to leave his job. At nine,
Virat was killed—a bullet to the head:
"He looked suspicious to me . . . glad he's dead."

V

He had to save the innocents from death,
    He heard their frantic cries for his protection.
He'd never stand down. To his final breath,
    Even if it demanded insurrection,
He would obey the higher law that saith,
    "Suffer the little children." No reflection
Was needed when he hit the detonator:
If he had faults, their faults were all the greater.

Harley. A Harley-Davidson motorbike.
AR-15. This semi-automatic rifle appeared to be the weapon of choice for the mass shootings that occurred with sickening regularity throughout the year.
"Suffer the little children". See Matthew 19:14.

VI

He had nothing against the blacks and Jews,
    The ones from India were kinda smart.
The Mexicans were everywhere, their crews
    Did all the work around there: A fresh start—
He understood that. But why did they choose
    His women? Each to his own kind was part
Of God's law. When he saw one with a white,
He knew that what he had to do was right.

VII

He didn't understand when customs changed:
    These crazy genders, diets, and gay marriage.
Who said the order should be rearranged,
    What was wrong with the horse before the carriage?
His children didn't call him, his estranged
    Wife took his money—they liked to disparage
What he believed in. He'd show who was boss:
One more dead bureaucrat was no one's loss.

VIII

Hell, let them come: the Black Hawks, Kevlar suits,
    The G-men, smoke-bombs, hand grenades, the lot.
For he was armed and ready. Thugs in boots
    Could kick his door down, but they would be shot.
He'd die his own man—from his corpse, the shoots
    Of a pure land would sprout, purged of the rot
Of mongrelism. Martyrdom would bring
Forward that hoped-for day: *Let freedom ring.*

Black Hawks. Black Hawk helicopters, bullet-proof vests made of Kevlar, and any federal agents (known as G-men) are the staples of paranoia about the military-industrial and national-security state that have animated the far right and far left for decades.

IX

Since when was it fair game to interject
　　When he was talking? When was it OK
To claim his privilege had to be "checked"?
　　For decades he'd worked hard, could he not say
Whatever he damn liked? Or not expect
　　Some deference? Chips would fall where they may,
But he would be allowed to speak right through,
Even if it required a death or two.

X

You once knew what it was to be a man.
　　You held a job; you put your kids through school;
You married someone organized who'd plan
　　Your life, but didn't change you. Then, the rule
Of law meant something and what you began
　　You finished. But these days you were a fool
If you did not take whatever you pleased.
The only "triggers" that mattered were squeezed.

XI

You women have to live with guys like these;
　　The ones who claim that might always makes right;
The ones who tie the nooses to the trees;
　　The hairy gutbucket and troglodyte
Who guns his oily hotrod; every sleaze
　　Who speaks of hard work, yet this parasite
Sucks at the creamy teats of state for free—
A champion of "real" liberty.

"Checked". This word and "triggers" are cooptations of "politically correct" speech regarding so-called "white privilege," the emotional abuse of minorities, and other aspects of the fight over the uses and abuses of rhetoric that have characterized attitudes towards race, gender, and language use on the political right and left in the last several years.

Troglodyte. A person holding ignorant or old-fashioned views.

XII

The entitled, condescending "voice of reason"
    Who shuts you up (because he knows what's best);
Who purrs, "For everything there is a season,"
    And yet year-round is feathering his nest;
Who loves to lecture you, though you've degrees in
    The subject, and when you start to protest,
Is flabbergasted there was a suggestion
That what he said might be open to question.

XIII

The idiot who catcalls in the street,
    Assuming that no lady can resist him,
As both of them offer the other "meat."
    And even though each woman has dismissed him,
He's confident (she's obviously in heat)
    Her ire is regret that she's not kissed him.
Or if not that, he's whiled away an hour
By showing females who has real power.

XIV

You'd thought that toxic masculinity—
    Unwarranted assurance, childish brashness,
Assertion without proof, misogyny,
    Indignant threats of retribution, rashness,
Bone-idleness, ass-backward sophistry,
    Refusal to back down, and talking trash—yes,
You hoped that after what we had endured
This adolescent country had matured.

"For everything there is a season". See Ecclesiastes 3:1.

XV

What naïfs you were to presume white guys
    Would take their place among the rest; how callow
To think they (we) would hand over the prize
    Awarded to them every day; how shallow
To hope they'd step down, and not exercise
    Each constitutional right. Having left fallow
(In their minds) the last eight years, they intended
Emasculated rule to be suspended.

XVI

How apt it is, therefore, that there appears
    A white man without conscience, heavenly
Mercy, or prudence, to dispel the tears
    That tremble inside masculinity;
A man who won't back down, openly leers
    At what he wants to fondle, cannot see
Beyond his own self-interest, who cares
Not one jot for any other's affairs.

XVII

A man who's never struggled, never fought
    For something he believes in. No grand mission
Has shaped his life, except what can be bought
    Or sold: without an atom of contrition,
Regret, or ruth; without a single thought
    Beyond the purview of an acquisition
To fortify the grandiosity
Of his labyrinthine monstrosity.

XVIII

And when the winding pathways of the maze
Come to an end, do you think you will find
A wounded, half-formed creature, who spends days
And nights howling for help? When you unwind
The skein of kindness, will his furious gaze
Soften. Thus, tempered, would he be inclined
To leave his darkness for the light of day,
And, raging, not turn inward or away?

XIX

I doubt it. The ungracious crenellations
(Amassed in eight jejune decades) grow stronger.
The buttressed grievances and crude foundations
Of ego are impermeable. The longer
The flippant palisades and battle stations
Stand to protect the male conceit, the wronger
We'll be in thinking that he'll be impeached:
This Bluebeard's castle's walls will not be breached.

XX

No decency escapes these parapets—
Just clouds of poisoned gas released each morning
To ruin moods for hours; curdled jets
Of nauseating tweets, rude and suborning.
You try to slough it off, read the regrets
From legislators impotently warning
"Stop!"—vainly pleading no good will come from it:
Yet wait a day . . . another stream of vomit.

Crenellations. Castle battlements.
Eight jejune decades. The current occupant of the White House has been building his simplistic emotional walls and battlements for over seventy years.
Bluebeard's castle. In addition to Bluebeard, I also allude in this segment to the labyrinth created by King Minos of Crete in which to house the mythical Minotaur. Both stories have been read psychologically as exempla of wounded masculinity and its fear of, and wish to control, the feminine.

XXI

For in the end, it's not about the voters.
　　Nor every issue he's feigned interest in.
It's not about the state of General Motors,
　　Or global trade, or (maybe) even skin.
It's not about whom he will pick for scotus,
　　Or finding out just who really did *win*.
It boils down to simple temperament:
This man is not fit to be president.

XXII

The only reason why he is still there
　　Is he's a man. Given what he has done,
If any woman decided to share
　　Her thoughts about a man's parts—oh what fun
The XY chromosomes would have! The air
　　Would go blue as they turned on her as one
And drummed her out of office for her sin:
It's certain that no woman'll ever win.

XXIII

He swims, unconscious, in the welcome waters
　　Of masculinity. The thirteen bros
Who drafted healthcare to affect all daughters,
　　Wives, mothers, sisters, and hurried to close
The clinics that would keep them healthy taught us
　　That "women's issues" simply do not pose
A problem to reflect on. Men believe
It's their job to determine who'll conceive.

General Motors. A common phrase regarding prosperity in mid-century America was, "As goes General Motors, so goes America."
scotus. Supreme Court of the United States.
Thirteen bros. The Senate committee convened by Majority Leader Mitch McConnell to write health-care legislation consisted of thirteen men and no women.

XXIV

What do they know of caring for the sick?
    Or looking after a disabled child
While working two jobs? Or when the dumb brick
    That used to be your husband went and filed
For bankruptcy to void his dues, his dick
    Lodged in another county seat, bills piled
High, you cannot afford to live . . . or sink. . . .
Do these men ever take the time to think

XXV

Of who cleans out their offices, or makes
    Their kids' beds, or rubs Brasso on their plates?
Of who comes in to brew their chai, or bakes
    Their croissants, or opens their enclave's gates?
Can they imagine what courage it takes
    To leave their lives behind and trust the fates
To seek freedom somewhere that's strange and new
Trusting what the U.S. proclaims is true?

XXVI

Or is it our shared task to ensure
    That these men know how much we are impressed
By how crucial they are, how much allure
    They have, and how we (the weak and distressed)
Are grateful they protect us? Then, demure
    Consumers, do we do our level best
To ignore their self-absorption and flip-flopping
By spending days and nights in online shopping?

XXVII

Whatever is the case, this frantic need
    Is more than a whole country could supply:
Think of his Cabinet, who went and peed
    Their pants in joy exclaiming how and why
They loved working for him. Each one agreed
    He was the greatest, while he cast his eye
Around the table like an emperor:
As if this was what government was for.

XXVIII

It's like the worst of white men's self-belief
    Is synthesized in one dude, and distilled:
Vanity, shamelessness, an endless beef
    With critics; coarseness; triteness; and a willed
Careless concupiscence. A leitmotif
    That runs throughout, and lets the tension build,
Is that beyond the lunacy, the drama:
How much he's plagued by hatred for Obama.

XXIX

But why pretend this lummox needs a cause
    To prosecute his dreadful, loathsome schemes?
The frantic efforts of staff to hit PAUSE,
    STOP, and RESTART will fail. The plaintive dreams
Of those who voted for him—his huge flaws
    Will snuff them out, and rend them at the seams
Because he doesn't care and never will:
You've been had and you will pick up the bill.

They loved working for him. The Cabinet meeting in question took place on June 13, 2017.

XXX

Those who still work for him—each ghastly day
    Brings yet another call for genuflection.
You stand before us, trying to display
    A shred of dignity, while your dejection
Is evident to everyone. He'll betray
    The little of what's left of your affection
And claim you were a tramp, a fraud, a loser:
Now is the time to fly from your abuser!

XXXI

Enough! Enough! Republicans be brave.
    Call for a special session and declare
The time has come for him to go. In grave,
    Regretful, rueful prose say this nightmare
Must end, and that the goal must be to save
    The country lest we fall into despair
And close up shop, for it will be too late
To rescue the scuppered vessel of state.

Scuppered. A vessel that has been deliberately holed so it will sink.

Canto VIII
August 2017

I

"This is my son, mine own Telemachus,
 To whom I leave the sceptre and the isle"—
Thus, Ulysses (from Tennyson). No wuss
 Was this princeling, but full of care and wile;
A stern-browed Ithacan (not treasonous),
 Who recognized that stringency and guile
(Not iffy courtiers from hostile nations)
Work best in furthering one's aspirations.

II

Together U & T hosed down the place
 Of oafish, lazy, good-for-nothing sons.
The ineffectual suitors, lacking grace,
 Had hung out there for years, consuming tons
Of food and wine and time. These wastes of space
 Were quickly flushed away to everyone's
Relief. Sometimes you'll find the worthless scion
Is tempered best when tickled with hot iron.

Ulysses. "Ulysses," line 33–34 by Alfred, Lord Tennyson (1809–1892).

III

Indulgence is the father to *this* man,
    His family, he pouts, is "quality."
What each day is revealing is his clan
    Has no more dignity or decency
Than *père*. The only difference I can
    Discern is that they don't appear to be
As desperate as father for attention,
Perhaps because he pays them a subvention.

IV

When I hear of a family of grifters,
    I think of card-sharks or someone's ex-spouse;
Of welfare slackers, inbred white-trash drifters,
    Or Mr. Skimpole sponging in *Bleak House*.
We know each family contains shoplifters,
    Dropouts, perverts, and mandatory souse.
That said, it's rare to find a group this cozy
Or dozy emulating Mafiosi.

V

At least the bloody Medicis had taste;
    The British monarchs patronized the Poet.
The Julio-Claudians weren't *all* debased,
    And while John Adams' progeny *did* blow it,
And Billy, Neil, Roger, *et al.* disgraced
    Their brothers, they at least had sense to show it
Mattered that bad behavior's repercussions
Should not mean selling us out to the Russians.

The British monarchs. William Shakespeare wrote for both Queen Elizabeth I and King
    James I. Since 1668, British monarchs have appointed a poet laureate.
Billy, Neil, Roger. Billy Carter, Neil Bush, and Roger Clinton. See *Dramatis Personae*.

VI

Lo, what is this we find? The first-born, Don,
　　Thought it would be a wizard wheeze to meet
With Putin flacks to set his paws upon
　　Some dish on Hillary. And to complete
The party? Jared Kushner, Putin's faun
　　Paul Manafort, and a lengthening sheet
Of scuzzballs. Now we see claims of collusion
Aren't just a liberal nighttime effusion.

VII

This Don is the same dude who loves to shoot
　　Whatever threatened or endangered beast
Wanders into his sights. The big galoot
　　Runs his pa's business, which means at the least
Should he and Eric prove less than astute
　　(A fair bet at the moment), then the greased
Duo will be themselves under the gun—
Something, for once, they won't find so much fun!

VIII

For evidently Mueller's closing in
　　On where the filthy lucre in this affair
Is found. Even ten rinse cycles of spin
　　Won't launder the rubles the Russian bear
Has dumped into his real estate. No "win"
　　Or even drummed-up international "scare"
Will cover up the fact from the word "Go"
He's been bought and propped up by Russian dough.

Russian bear. The symbol of the Russian state is the bear.

IX

That's why he has withheld his tax releases,
       That's why he gins up his bromance with Vlad;
That's why he'll let the U.S. fall to pieces
       Rather than stiff *these* clients. His comrade
And cronies have unloaded piles of feces
       Upon their greatest fan. Our Stalingrad
Will happen when, at the appropriate minute,
Vlad flips the switch and we are buried in it.

X

To stop this shit storm, what did Don propose
       To stink-proof some of the executive suite?
Did Junior even feign to hold his nose
       As he ceded Ukraine, said they'd defeat
The sanctions, or adopt the quid pro quos
       That Russia wanted? And what coded tweet
Or speech did Pops give to let his Vlad know
That it was clear who *really* ran the show?

XI

What's so unusual in this concern
       Is that it isn't sleuths or great reporting
That's lending us these insights. What we learn
       Does not emerge from haggard journos sorting
Through trashcans, or a much-abused intern.
       No D.C. madam or sting with coke-snorting
Is causing 45 to come a cropper:
It's coming from within the White House proper.

Stalingrad. The Siege of Stalingrad during World War II proved a turning point for the Germans in the cost of lives and matériel. It is now a byword for a heavy defeat.
Ukraine. Forces aligned with Russia, as well as Russian soldiers, invaded and occupied Crimea and eastern Ukraine in the years following the toppling of Ukrainian president Viktor Yanukovych in February 2014.

XII

Are junior staffers huddling in nooks
    Lowering their tones as the boss walks by?
Are they scribbling down notes so that their books
    Will capture the dysfunction? Do they lie
To please him or avoid the dirty looks
    Of other liars? When the F.B.I.
Hauls them to court will they stick to their brief,
Or tell you they were mimicking the chief?

XIII

Of this we can be sure: this nest of vipers
    Has poisoned government for a decade.
You huddle by your desk frightened that snipers
    Will pick you off, that any random aide
Will throw you to the wolves: being one-stripers
    Is thankless when you're so often betrayed.
Who'd work in that place even for a week,
When what you hold dear is undone by pique?

XIV

You think about it: what marginal action
    For good can be achieved when day by day
You're undermined? Each project has no traction
    Because you can't set out a play-by-play
Without him wrecking it. Meanwhile, each faction
    Pits you against your colleagues—what they say
About you ends up in the press. Each morning
Should be prefaced with a government warning.

XV

Sean Spicer (R.I.P.) detests "The Mooch,"
    Who really wants to be the Chief of Staff.
Reince Priebus thinks the old man's latest pooch
    Is a mere showboat and good for a laugh.
Jared-Ivanka love his coif and smooch—
    And papa's happy. Plus, on their behalf,
If they can piss off Bannon, then it's more
Likely that Daddy will show him the door.

XVI

There's old Jeff Sessions with the dunce's hat,
    Because he did not do what he desired.
And Sarah Sanders will hear that she's fat:
    His way of telling women that they're fired.
The whole crew will soon end up a doormat
    On which he wipes his feet when he grows tired
Of them obeying rules, laws, inner compasses,
Instead of diving into endless rumpuses.

XVII

You wouldn't know this White House has got "weeks"
    To focus on issues and policies.
The reason is outbursts and frequent leaks
    Consume the media's bland nobodies
And color his proposals. Such bespeaks
    His odd impairments and iniquities
That lets him sabotage what he holds dear
As if achievement is a kind of smear.

"**The Mooch**". White House Communications Director Anthony Scaramucci's nickname.

Dunce's hat. The current occupant of the White House expressed considerable unease with the performance of Attorney General Jeff Sessions for not doing more to stave off the investigation into Russian meddling in the election and, most particularly, the G.O.P. candidate's presidential campaign.

XVIII

I never glimpse a genuine concession
  To joy or pleasure, just obnoxious gloating.
I never get an inkling or impression
  That he likes something for its sake—like floating
On air or oceanic bliss. Aggression,
  Derision, shtick, and humbug before doting
Admirers seem to be what he most needs:
Sucking the lifeblood out of which he feeds.

XIX

What's left is but a broken, hollow shell,
  A fractured carapace for president.
He doesn't make you trust all will be well
  If we believed in him. Instead, torment
And hatred, twenty-seven kinds of hell
  Ensue from each obnoxious tweet he's sent.
He's not struggling against another foe.
It's simple: He's the *fons et origo*.

XX

Consider that last month he spoke before
  Thousands of Boy Scouts at their jamboree.
He could have eulogized esprit de corps,
  Steadfastness, discipline, fidelity;
Hailed sacrifice and usefulness—the lore
  That Boy Scouts live by. But, this nobody
Addressed a Friars Roast, without restraint,
Full not of motivation but complaint.

Fons et origo. Latin tag: "Fountain and origin of."
Thousands of Boy Scouts. Forty-five's speech before the Boy Scouts of America on July 24, 2017, was widely lamented as ill-conceived and inappropriate.
Friars Roast. A raucous evening of comedic speeches that insult the guest of honor.

XXI

Still harping on crowds at the Inauguration,
    Lamenting how the health-care bill is stalled,
Threatening folks in his administration,
    Railing again at fake news, he recalled
How he won (state by state) throughout the nation.
    Then he held every teenager enthralled
As he recounted how a billionaire
Bought a big boat to hold his "parties" there.

XXII

Perhaps he thought the lads would find the swingers
    And moneybaggers people to admire.
Or had in mind that such ribald humdingers
    Would light under these lusty youths a fire
And turn them into debt-laden right-wingers:
    Rich wise guys with a babe whom they can hire
To decorate the prow and mix the drinks,
Or guard the rugrats while they hit the links.

XXIII

He thanked the children for their votes and told them
    They could sing "Merry Christmas" once again.
He criticized Obama, and then sold them
    His tax repatriation ploy; made plain
He thought D.C. a "sewer," and cajoled them
    To promise they'd not let their mojo wane.
In sum, the only point of his address
Was to convince himself of his success.

Still harping on crowds. When it was demonstrated that the crowd for the Inauguration ceremony in Washington in January 2017 was considerably smaller than for the same event in 2008, 45 complained of media distortion.

Moneybaggers. A portmanteau word combining "moneybags" and "carpetbaggers."

"Merry Christmas". Fox News, particularly Bill O'Reilly, has long argued each holiday season that secular liberals are campaigning to "destroy" Christmas.

XXIV

Maybe he thought teen boys would understand
    The ebbing, flagging powers, need to win.
Or that he hoped the scouts would lend a hand
    And help this pensioner through thick and thin.
Like everything he does, it wasn't planned
    And his neuroses bled through his bronzed skin
Onto the tens of thousands ranked below
Who knew that, at the least, they'd catch a show.

XXV

And, in the end, are we not entertained?
    The meltdowns, hissy fits, unchecked compulsion,
Potemkin signings, morning rants, harebrained
    Ideas, and veneering and emulsion
From panderers and peddlers, have retrained
    Our sense of wrong, relaxing our revulsion
By turning abnormality quotidian
And painting self-reflection deep obsidian.

XXVI

It feels like things are coming to a head.
    I am aware that the much-yearned-for end
Has been deferred and many tears been shed
    At thoughts this presidency may extend
To a full term, and further. So, I tread
    With caution when my thesis I defend:
I cannot think this can go on much more
Without him simply blowing up the store.

Potemkin. Fake event, situation, or location staged for political purposes.
Veneering. A reference to the shallow social climbers, the Veneerings, in Charles Dickens'
    Our Mutual Friend (1865).

XXVII

He clearly wants Jeff Sessions to resign.
    He urgently hopes Bob Mueller will cease.
You sense he's jonesing to can Rosenstein
    If only to acquire a moment's peace.
"I s'pose," he thinks, "it would be asinine
    To do any of these, lest they release
A crisis that I simply won't survive."
These are some of the thoughts of 45.

XXVIII

"Now hold on," he replies, "if Sessions goes
    I'll employ Giuliani—he's my chum.
Instead of weak-willed Price and his bozos
    I could get Newt. He'd love to stick his thumb
In Ryan's eyes, McConnell's face. Just shows:
    Go with the bruisers who can ruck and scrum.
They love me and they'll never let me down,
Not like the G.O.P. in this dumb town."

XXIX

Can you imagine? How would this enhance
    The G.O.P. among the younger set?
What image would it mold or cause advance
    Except to make millennials regret
That they'd survived to see this day? Fat chance
    That either nominee would pass. And yet,
He'd name Ted Cruz for A.G., as a wheeze,
To have him beg for favors on his knees.

Jonesing. Slang for craving, as an addiction.
A. G. Attorney General.

XXX

Given this crisis, Democrats' chief tenet
    Should in the midterms in 2018
Be to win back the House and/or the Senate
    And not take anything as read. We've seen
What condescension does for parties—when it
    Demands a sharp and principled machine
To send as many people to the polls
And wrest back at least one of the controls.

XXXI

Let's not be coy about this. Self-protection
    Is what he cares about. If he must drag
Congress along the floor as misdirection
    Then he won't hesitate. If a false flag
Is needed, he will raise it. No abjection
    Is too much; each supporter's body bag
Is waiting to be zipped if they assent
To *this* ask: "Will you serve the president?"

Canto IX

September 2017

I

Satire depends for its effectiveness
    Upon the supposition a way through
Ineptitude, aggressiveness, and mess
    Can be discerned; that what is good and true
Is evident to all those who profess
    To be the thoughtful, decent person who
Knows right from wrong, feels empathy and shame,
And seeing evil, calls it by its name.

II

Since his election, I've been mostly sickened
    And stunned in equal measure. I have tried
To understand those whose bruised hearts were quickened
    By his excess, who felt that they'd been lied
Enough to, who enjoyed that he'd no slick and
    Genteel stump speech; and worried that the tide
Was running out—so they gave him their vote:
He'd tip the ship, sure; but he'd float their boat.

III

I'm not unsympathetic to the claim
 That the elites get more than their fair share;
That for the working stiff, the social game
 Is rigged against him; those who say they "care"
Don't understand the pressures; that the blame
 Goes to both parties; and that one's despair
At straight-talker, glib hack, or bland patrician
Makes one vote for an anti-politician.

IV

Through flimflam, insolence, and the deceit
 He's sullied us with; through each simpering flob
And pestilential snot-stream that each tweet
 Smears over us; through the pain this fat slob
Inflicts on us each day, I've tried to meet
 His voters halfway. But no more, this yob
Has not my pledge, and nor should he from you:
If you cared for this land, you'd say so, too.

V

Roll up! "The Mooch" was fired from the cannon,
 His brief role in the circus done and dusted.
Priebus was shown the exit, and Steve Bannon
 (The conjurer of smoke and mirrors) busted.
The bogus ringmaster remains: the man on
 Whom all this nonsense hangs. These dipsticks trusted
That they would have his ear, be in the know.
What fools! For treachery is his m.o.

Flob. British slang for sputum.
Snot. British slang for mucus.
Yob. British slang for a lout.
M.o. *Modus operandi* (Latin), or "way of working."

VI

Sebastian Gorka, the soiled-goods hawker,
    Has gone. He blames the enemies inside
The White House: saboteurs, says this big talker,
    And would-be Democrats, who have denied
The big "creep" (aka Hillary's stalker)
    His nationalist agenda. You decide
Just whether the head barker needs a hand
In ruining his "vision" for this land.

VII

He neither wants to learn or work or read.
    He's idle, ignorant, and apathetic;
Attacks the very people that he'll need
    To get things done. Yet, like a forced emetic,
Or a medieval quack who wants to bleed
    The sick body to cure it, or ascetic
Who hopes *gnosis* emerges from starvation,
The enema of the people scours the nation.

VIII

And there is something cleansing, I confess it,
    In what he's forcing us to expurgate.
A boil or cyst—no matter how we dress it—
    Must at some point be drained. And just to wait
And hope it goes away (rather than press it)
    Will only let it ooze and suppurate.
His sickening and poisonous derision
Has made on legion lesions an incision.

Hillary's stalker. During the debates in 2016, the G.O.P. nominee for president routinely
    invaded Hillary Clinton's personal space. She later referred to him as a "creep."
Gnosis. Greek word for "knowledge" or "enlightenment."

IX

Just what is it emerging from the stew?
　　What mucilaginous and rancid chunk
Of undigested hate plops into view?
　　What seborrheic pustule has this punk
Squeezed with his tiny fingers? What moist poo
　　Dribbles from his fat cheeks? What slimy gunk
Infects the public sphere, backs up the pipes?
And leaves us a despoiled stars and stripes?

X

What sooty spittle's foaming on the tongue?
　　What melanomas bloom upon the skin?
What oily film that coated either lung
　　Has been hacked forth to tar each double chin?
What pungent rash has now (unbidden) sprung,
　　And made us sweat and pullulates within?
(Is part of this disgraceful concentration
The shameful verse that forms this compilation?)

XI

What rotten wind's been loosened from the bowels?
　　What halitotic eructation freed?
What mucky bin of sanitary towels
　　Or skidmarked underwear stained with old seed
Has been left out, unwashed, and now befouls
　　The air? What scabby, loathsome demon breed
Stumble like moldy zombies through our streets?
Clad in their polo shirts and slacks not sheets?

Mucilaginous. Thick and gluey.
Seborrheic. Itchy and flaky.
Pullulates. Spreads.
Halitotic. Suffering from bad breath.
Eructation. A belch.

XII

Fascists, that's who. Them and the KKK,
    The neo-Nazis, and the alt-right crowd.
These men (and women) act as if it's they
    Who are the honorable ones—the avowed
Custodians of what's good—whose rebel gray
    Should rise again and don the whitewashed shroud.
What it required was autocratic hacks
To wrest the country from the Jews and blacks.

XIII

And now they've found their leaders. One, Jeff Sessions,
    Is poised to once more lock up black men ("thugs")
To make the world safe for those whose transgressions
    Are white collar in every sense. On drugs
(Also again) he'll wage war, with concessions
    I'm sure for most whites (poor or rich). The jug's
For criminals, as long as they aren't armed
With licensed guns. *They*'ll walk the streets unharmed.

XIV

We've known a long time of the other guy,
    He's shown his racial animus for years.
His father loved the Klan, and it's clear why
    He asked about Obama's birthplace: fears
About a black man wielding power lie
    Behind the sell-out Giuliani's jeers
That Obama loved not America.
And now we have the black-clad Antifa.

Jug. Slang for prison.
Giuliani's jeers. Republican Rudolph Giuliani claimed that President Barack Obama didn't
    love America during a speech in February 2015.

XV

This is the game the right wing likes to play.
    To set up some equivalence, sow doubt.
"We may have lynched," they cry, "but every day
    The blacks kill one another! And you shout
Insults as we practice free speech; you say
    It's hate, and so do we of you. My lout
Is matched by yours—and each one's views are awful.
But if there is no violence, it's lawful."

XVI

These views can (if you squint hard) be appealing,
    Play to a moderate's dreams of liberty:
That in the public marketplace, freewheeling
    Ideas on how much of history
To hold and what to let go, what is healing
    And what is harmful, are calmed in degree
By letting the extremes of left and right
Have at each other in an endless fight.

XVII

Or if not that, then people of good sense
    Will come together in the solid center.
That the two parties will expunge the offense
    Caused by their flanks and raise up a big tent, a
Response to those who'd argue that defense
    Against anarcho-fascists, to present a
Bold front against them, are most necessary
To guarantee the future's not so scary.

XVIII

But what if the habitual restraint
    Shown by the president just isn't there?
What if one party's craven, its complaint
    Too muted, or complacent, doctrinaire?
What if it's calculated that the quaint
    Notions of normalcy—even to care
About society—aren't worth the sweat?
Do they think they can temporize the threat?

XIX

Is each Republican scared of attacks
    Not just from him but Breitbart? Will they bow
And supine lie upon their spineless backs
    To take his bullying? Will they kowtow
Because the diehard right will send out flacks
    To threaten or condemn should they not vow
Allegiance to the feckless autocrat?
And if they do so, will that then be that?

XX

They say that it will *never* get so far.
    Someone will say, "Have you no decency?"
And like McCarthy his ascendant star
    Will fall, and he'll resign or cease to be
Of consequence? But it's beyond bizarre
    That nothing that he does will shake the tree
Of true believers or the timid shills
Who will stay with him (even if he kills).

Temporize. To avoid making a decision to gain time.
Breitbart. Breitbart News: an online organ of the far right.
McCarthy. Senator Joseph McCarthy's House Unamerican Activities Committee (H.U.A.C.) was brought to an end in 1954 when Joseph Welch, an attorney for the U.S. Army, which was under investigation, asked McCarthy, "Have you no sense of decency?"
Even if he kills. During the election campaign, the eventual G.O.P. candidate said that he could kill someone and still not lose the base of his support.

XXI

Despite his spite, his knavery and gall,
    He yet retains the love of some one-third
Of voters: those who want to build the Wall;
    Who itch for phantom former greatness; heard
In the attacks upon the elites a call
    For dreams that were theirs but had been deferred
By immigrants and spongers, and their sort,
Whom their man would imprison or deport.

XXII

Since Charlottesville, and Heather Heyer's death
    (Mown down by an alt-right supremacist),
We've barely had a chance to draw a breath
    Without his calumny, flick-of-the-wrist
Contempt for truth, or tossed-off shibboleth
    To show he "cares." He acts royally pissed
When his equivocations and neurosis
Reveal more evidence of his psychosis.

XXIII

My anger's not about the monuments
    To Jim Crow, Southern history, states rights.
It's how it's "us" or "them," blatant defense
    That those who march with Nazis are the knights
Who should (and must) defend "us." It's pretense
    That "heritage" is colorblind, that whites
And blacks will obviously vote with their races:
Why unify us when we've our places?

Charlottesville. Activist Heather Heyer was killed on August 13, 2017 while protesting a gathering of neo-Nazis in Charlottesville, Virginia. The shock that such a gathering should take place, that someone would be killed, and that 45 equivocated on who was to blame and that there were "good people on both sides," plunged the nation into a conversation about race, politics, and the legacy of the South.

Shibboleth. A defining idea or outmoded principle.

XXIV

Listen, supporters! He's clearly unfit.
    He won't do what you want, because he can't
Do what is needed to get any shit
    Done. He's undisciplined; can only rant
When smooth persuasion beckons; throws a fit
    When smarts would open doors, and offers scant
Examples of the skill that, brick by brick,
Builds coalitions that make D.C. tick.

XXV

But these deficiencies pale next to others:
    His default is to stimulate dissension.
It's obvious that if he had his druthers
    He'd end the opposition and convention.
He yearns for battle—brothers against brothers—
    As long as he can bathe in the attention.
If it is vulgar, conflict-rich, and scrappy,
And TV ratings break the roof, he's happy.

XXVI

But even *this* description makes it seem
    As though there's art behind his brash persona.
A cunning scheme to drain the swamp? The dream
    Of a revived America? Each donor
To his campaign to get a favored scheme
    Fast-tracked to nowhere? Nonsense. A rank stoner,
Blissed out and clueless, would detect this rat
As someone who's no cattle and all hat.

Drain the swamp. A phrase used during rallies in the G.O.P. nominee's 2016 campaign to describe removing timeservers, special interests, lobbyists, and other professional politicians from the halls of power.

No cattle and all hat. To be "all hat and no cattle," is to be all talk and no substance.

XXVII

And, apropos, the monumental flood
    That Harvey has poured onto Houston, Tex.,
Gives him still yet another chance to blood
    Himself as useful and unselfish, flex
His presidential muscle. To the mud
    He then could bid farewell, as he projects
The image of a leader, reconciler,
And not a canting, serial defiler.

XXVIII

He could proclaim an era of resilience
    In facing climate change; free up resources,
Imagination, and people of brilliance
    To shape the next five decades, so the forces
Of nature might be softened, a consilience
    Of Texas grit and focus that divorces
Us finally from fossil fuels and coal
And stops us digging holes and makes us whole.

XXIX

Yeah, right! If you think he'll do such a thing
    Then I've a bridge in Brooklyn that's for sale.
The presidency amplifies to bring
    The true man to the fore (it's still just male).
And so it's proved. Houston will no more sting
    His conscience than a dog will catch its tail.
He'll get his photo-op and let the state
Clean up the mess, and claim that he's done great.

Harvey. Hurricane Harvey caused widespread flooding that devastated Houston, Texas, and the environs in August 2017.
Canting. Hypocritical.
Consilience. An agreement between disciplines.

XXX

Houston's a diverse place, it represents
    America in microcosm. Here's
The first great litmus test: This president's
    High Noon, the whole ball game: it's endless tears
Or acclamation. Handling such events
    Is how a nation calibrates its fears
And aspirations for their families:
Will he lift up or bring us to our knees?

High Noon. A 1952 film starring Grace Kelly and Gary Cooper, in which a marshal defends a town against a gang of criminals with no help from his fellow citizens.

Canto X

October 2017

I

I first flew here in 1987,
    Landing expectantly at JFK.
It was December, and the vault of heaven,
    As I recall it, was not English gray
But liquid blue. I felt my spirit leaven
    As from the Carey Bus I stepped that day
To feel the echoed beat of dancing feet
Near Grand Central on 42nd Street.

II

I knew right then I'd come back here to live,
    My union with the city felt organic.
The pace, the noise, the hustle didn't give
    Me pause. Instead, they had a groovy, manic
And syncopated kick; a combative
    Yet welcoming impatience; a galvanic,
Persistent pulse that swung and throbbed: ambition
Was all that was required for admission.

JFK. John F. Kennedy International Airport in Queens, New York.
"Beat of dancing feet". Lyrics from *42nd Street*, the long-running musical by Harry Warren,
    based on a 1933 film and other sources.

III

Transferring to the U.S. was, for me,
    A break from past restraints of class and clan,
A chance to get a job and to breathe free
    Without assumptions of what sort of man
A person of my background had to be.
    No one cared where I went to school, my plan
Needed no pulling of the old-boy strings,
Political alignments, or such things.

IV

Naturlich, I have had enormous luck:
    My gender, race, accent, and education.
I'm tall, I'm able-bodied, and don't suck
    At sports; a common sexual orientation
Is mine, and though I can still be a schmuck,
    I try to honor each friend and relation,
As well as strangers that I meet, with fairness,
Kindness, and decency, or plain awareness.

V

I, therefore, know my views are rarified:
    That N.Y.C. is not the U.S.A.
I try to be as honest and clear-eyed
    About how much Great Britain falls away
From its view of itself; how people died
    Directly for my comfort. The U.K.
Has still not reckoned with its shameful past,
And that is wrong. That silence must not last.

VI

So, I'm aware I'm not much of a guide
    To my new-found-land. And I cannot know
What life must feel like when you are denied
    Full liberty because of race, although
Your people built the nation. I decide
    To what I pledge allegiance, and can go
Wherever I wish. My views, newly minted,
Perforce must be both blinkered and rose-tinted.

VII

When I came here to live, in '91,
    The days were dark: the murder rate was high,
The city's mood was grim. And yet the sun
    Still rose and people worked, and, by and by,
With more cops on the street, and CompStat run,
    The death toll fell, although the reasons why
Remain uncertain. We may never know
Why homicides have plummeted so low.

VIII

Perhaps an increase in incarcerations;
    Consolidation of the trade in crack;
Removal of lead paint from installations
    So kids could stay in school and keep on track;
Sickened by death, young men left altercations
    With no cold body on the hot tarmac:
Each change contributed—to which, add one:
The state tried to control who got a gun.

My new-found-land. See John Donne's "To His Mistress Going to Bed," line 27.

CompStat. The analysis of comparative crime statistics allowed police to target high-crime areas, and adopt tactics to address the violence.

Why homicides. Some pointed to the city's policy of stopping large numbers of young men (mainly of color) and frisking them for weapons. This thesis has been questioned: since the ending of "stop and frisk" in 2014, crime has continued to fall.

IX

The longer that I live here, it grows clearer
    To me how hurt this country is, how cracked.
Elections pass, laws change, but we're no nearer
    To addressing the sad truth that the compact
On race–class, North–South (which a thin veneer, a
    Mask of politeness hides), an artifact
Of our virgin birth, is now a curse,
Which, since we cannot deal with it, grows worse.

X

Yet when I think of this place I call home
    I feel more pity, bafflement, than rage.
I revel in not having far to roam
    To greet the world, and thereby to engage
With awe at how this city's polychrome
    Environment works as a kind of stage
Where we each play a part. Diversity
Can never be a shortcoming to me.

XI

This month, I've binge-watched the ten episodes
    Of Ken Burns' series on the Vietnam War.
You see how each choice, fault, and lie erodes
    The confidence, faith, and the moral core
Of those sucked in—how every action bodes
    Ill, and a deep shame is confirmed. It tore
Apart whole nations, people, families,
The ordinary grunts, and Vietnamese.

"**We each play a part**". See Shakespeare's *As You Like It*, II, vii, 138f.
Grunts. GIs.

XII

The wall that Maya Lin designed let pain
 And grief emerge as you descended in.
We need to plumb that fury, and not feign
 Either contempt or smugness. No threat-grin
Should censor folks who sorrow for the slain,
 However they were killed. We must begin
To face the horrors of the past, not let
Us fool ourselves it's better to forget.

XIII

It seems to me that one way we're unwell,
 Is how and why we've fetishized the gun:
A symbol of resistance, pride, a gel
 That holds a tribe together; how a son
Shows Dad he is a man. No tolling bell
 Can break the itchy trigger that someone
Who buys a weapon, swearing not to abuse it,
Will at some point feel that he's *forced* to use it.

XIV

Yet, when a shooter murders fifty-nine
 Attendees at a concert in Las Vegas,
I wonder if perhaps the fault is mine,
 As a non-native, thinking that guns plague us;
Not getting that guns are a piquant sign
 Of rural life, freedom, the way a magus
Might brandish his wand and make disappear
The maladies of disrespect and fear.

Shooter murders fifty-nine. On October 1, 2017, a gunman opened fire from a Las Vegas hotel on a group of concert-goers, killing dozens and wounding hundreds of others. He eventually took his own life. No motive has yet been discovered.

XV

I understand the Founders' deep alarm
 About an over-reaching central state.
The fragile army needed men to arm
 Themselves to combat threats, both small and great,
From foreign foes. I do not get the charm
 Of shooting animals for fun, but rate
Such pastimes not as bad as factory farming:
That's nothing but a crucible for harming.

XVI

I guess a gun can make you feel more safe
 When you live in the sticks. An indoor range
I've shot in, and I think that it would chafe
 A sane gun owner (or he'd find it strange)
That anyone would think it cool to strafe
 Whoever comes in view. But this exchange
Is not permissible. The N.R.A.
Rules Congress, and it will not go away.

XVII

Australia once felt a similar pain
 And banned some guns and deaths declined a lot.
When sixteen kids were cut down in Dunblane
 Restrictions were imposed. Of course, it's not
As if you cannot kill; and an insane
 Person will find a way. It's just it got
A little harder to commit the crime:
More lives were spared because it bought some time.

N.R.A.. The National Rifle Association.
Australia. Following a mass shooting in Port Arthur, Australia, in 1996, the government
 drastically reduced the number of guns in circulation.
Dunblane. The murder of eighteen people, including children, in Dunblane, Scotland, in
 1996 led to restrictions on guns in the U.K.

XVIII

But not here, not in these United States.

    How can this be the price of liberty?

The opioid addiction rightly rates

    As a crisis of public health; how free

Can we be when so many die? What straits

    Will make us see what other nations see?

We're killing one another in the streets

Whether we are (or not) wearing white sheets.

XIX

Not even 45 is, thus, to blame

    For these old wounds, he merely rubs more salt in.

We like to think he is the worst, but shame

    Is yours and mine, whoever we find fault in.

We're equally wrong in playing the game

    Of thinking that we're more evolved. A halt in

Believing we're untainted is what's needed,

If we're to heal the body that we've bleeded.

XX

So, murder, guilt, and controversy reigns

    While seismic happenings are underway.

It's possible the ulcers and migraines

    That he inflicts upon us every day

Disguise a worse disease: that our veins

    Are being emptied while we hope and pray

For health. But all he does suggests this man

Has no clue: that he doesn't have a plan.

XXI

And yet it's also true that great events
 Are cooking slowly, and we are distracted.
Even if we swapped him for VP Pence
 Occurrences would still leave us impacted.
The elite have failed us terribly, and hence,
 When dreadful laws are forcibly enacted
To make survival possible, we'll know
We blew the chances not so long ago.

XXII

Season of mists and mellow fruitfulness
 This ain't. Each tempest and disastrous flood
Makes plain that nature's might can deliquesce
 Each well-formed thought and road; the viscous mud
Tugs at the hopes and knees, and in the mess
 Brings progress down to earth with a great thud.
These storms, while often vivid and climactic,
Serve as a kind of mental prophylactic.

XXIII

For they are not the main things we should fear.
 Beneath the placid, ordinary day
Just slightly warmer than the previous year;
 Or springs the wettest yet; or early May
Experiencing record temps; severe
 Drought, fire, or monsoon—the primrose way
To hell is being paved in each meridian,
Until the terrible event's quotidian.

Seasons of mists and mellow fruitfulness. The first line of John Keats' "Ode to Autumn."
Deliquesce. Liquefy.
Primrose way. An adaptation of "the primrose path to the everlasting bonfire," spoken by
 the Porter in William Shakespeare's *Macbeth*, II, iii.

XXIV

Will folklorists describe how massive storms
    That ripped apart the entire hemisphere,
Or hurricanes that overrode the norms
    Of only months before, caused to appear
An armed resistance to the rumored swarms
    Of homeless migrants crossing each frontier,
Leading to martial law, rule by decree,
And tyranny from sea to shining sea?

XXV

We are already well beyond the dawn
    Of loss and disappearance. Gradually,
We notice birds, mammals, and fish are gone
    While we run through our tired repartee
Of just how we are the *sine qua non*,
    The life worthy of life, the apogee
Of the Almighty's vision. Each statistic
Suggests a self-importance that's hubristic.

XXVI

Will poets tell the unbelieving youth
    That once there roamed across a fertile earth
Tigers and rhinos, and ("It is the truth!")
    White bears and elephants; that once their worth
Was measured by a skin or horn or tooth,
    And so we slaughtered them? And when the dearth
Of fish was something we could not ignore,
We carried on until there were no more.

Sea to shining sea. See "God Bless America," by Irving Berlin.
Sine qua non. Latin tag meaning "without which none" or "essential element."

XXVII

The places of the world will vanish, too—
    Submerged or just abandoned. Holy sites:
Where life and death took our forebears through
    The generations; where the annual rites
That marked time's passage, formed the social glue,
    And brought us joy were held. No fancy flights
Of virtual reality will sate
The mourning when we find it is too late.

XXVIII

At this pace, though, we'll not live long enough
    To rue just what we have and haven't done.
The U.S.–D.P.R.K. thugs talk tough
    Threaten to make things warmer than the sun
By blowing us to smithereens—the stuff
    Of nightmares realized. A megaton
Of death that blows ten million to bits
Because these damaged men are having fits.

XXIX

As ever, making worse the already bad,
    The C-in-C mocks Tillerson at State.
Each time I've named a person who has had
    A role in this farce, they find that the date
Of their appointment has elapsed. This lad
    Is likely to go next—a bit too late
To save his reputation. Stick a fork (a
Tine or two at the least) into Bob Corker.

XXX

Before we know it, we'll be off, once more,
    To war, and—lo!—we'll see the nation rally.
A trope as old as time, we'll count the score
    In bodies, and decide what sort of tally
We can call victory. Once more, the poor
    Will suffer most from every bombing sally
That we set forth on. Once more, an erasure
Of unknown, nameless thousands in East Asia.

XXXI

Will we step back and pause, weigh up the odds,
    Think of a longer future than next tweet?
Or will we merely shrug and hope that God's
    A destiny for us? Will the drumbeat
Be too loud to resist? Will our squads
    Square off against each other in the street?
Before year's end will we love Uncle Sam?
Or find ourselves reliving Vietnam?

Canto XI

November 2017

I

It's been twelve months since I cast my first vote
    For president, and rose a sadder guy
The morrow morn. It's been a year of note,
    Mainly because the many reasons why
Shit happened are lethal to touch. No rote
    Political response can quantify
The social pathogens that marinate,
Mutate, and spread within this wretched state.

II

A white man with a grievance and a gun
    Has once more taken lives; bromides and prayers
Have been delivered; nothing will be done.
    In days, another will stare through crosshairs
And murder more good men and women, one
    Who wouldn't hurt a fly. But then, who cares?
Let people kill themselves and think they're free,
As long as I'm not in the mortuary.

The morrow morn. An adaptation of the last two lines of Samuel Taylor Coleridge's "Rime of the Ancient Mariner."

Once more taken lives. On November 15, 2017, a man shot up a Texas church, killing twenty-six people.

III

Is the U.S. a beacon anymore?
    Do people *really* reason if they arm
Themselves that they can even out the score,
    Or at the least protect themselves from harm?
It's like we imagine marching off to war
    Means fewer maimed and dead. I'll bet the farm
That we'll be dodging bullets in the street
Fired by Nazi addicts packing heat.

IV

Meanwhile, the calls for doing something fade,
    No policies are brought up for debate.
No money is allotted, while the frayed
    And broken kinfolk desperately wait
For some sign that they haven't been betrayed
    Again. To lessen just a bit the rate
Of death, might Congress summon up the will
To pass even an unimportant bill?

V

It's not as if we didn't get how sick
    And feverish we were the last eight years.
The self-congratulation and the shtick
    Of the '08 election—when the tears
Of everyone would dry (as if a quick
    Volte-face could undercut systemic fears)—
Proved premature and arrogant: they rested
On self-indulgence that had not been tested.

VI

We get the politics that we deserve:
    The folderol, the pettiness, the lies,
The stupid pieties, failures of nerve,
    The grandstanding, the cutting down to size,
The odium, the donor-lobbies' verve
    In grabbing what they can, the faux surprise
At felonies and graft. One antidote?
Getting one's fat ass off the couch to vote.

VII

This month this obvious fact was proven true,
    When Democrats came to the polls en masse.
Electors voted for contenders who
    Rebuked the casual malice of a crass
And stupid vagabond, without a clue.
    From every region, gender, shape, and class
They came: they even voted for (*Hosanna!*)
A black man to be mayor in Montana!

VIII

It's true, one should admit that these successes
    Don't demonstrate the Democratic Party
Is ready for primetime. No random guesses
    Or fiendish cleverness of Moriarty
Are necessary to conclude that stresses
    Of life with 45 led to the hearty
Rebuff of the G.O.P. through the land.
That's something Democrats must understand.

Black man. Wilmot Collins, a Liberian-American, was elected the mayor of Helena, Montana, on November 8, 2017.

Cleverness of Moriarty. Professor Moriarty is the cunning arch-enemy of detective Sherlock Holmes in many of Arthur Conan Doyle's novels and short stories.

IX

We've now learned that the bankrupt D.N.C.

 Was last year in hock to Clinton's campaign,

Which shows how center-leftists fail to see

 That power matters, yes, but the terrain

Is broad, and each municipality

 Offers the chance for candidates to gain

Proficiency and skills, and put a dent

In the great reach of any president.

X

Yet, when I hope the net is closing in,

 The sands of time are (at last) running out—

That Deep Throat's gargled, and will soon begin

 To tell us where the money is; that Doubt

Has sunk her claws into his orange skin

 And scrapes away his ego's mildewed grout

That keeps the rot concealed—we let him find

Another way to stupefy the mind.

XI

I watched last month as that milquetoast Jeff Flake

 Denounced the president. The Arizonan

Hardly caused any senators to shake

 In their expensive, tasseled shoes; no Conan

Was he, cutting a swathe; more a cupcake

 Than poisoned pill deliverer. To phone in

We've now learned. In her 2017 book, *Hacks*, Democratic political consultant and pundit Donna Brazile wrote that the Democratic Party was so short of money in 2015 and 2016 that it used money from Hillary Clinton's campaign.

Deep Throat. The name given to F.B.I. special agent Mark Felt (1913–2008), the government insider who provided important information to journalists about the Watergate scandal. The name comes from a pornographic movie popular at the time.

Conan. Conan the Barbarian, a heavily muscled warrior popularized in a 1982 movie of the same name by Arnold Schwarzenegger.

125

A quasi-resignation counts as mettle
Only when you have really grasped the nettle.

XII

Since then a pallid cavalcade of geezers
    Have said they've had enough. Their worried spouses
Have sternly called back home these would-be Caesars
    To sit on boards and eat lunch at clubhouses,
Rather than be the febrile buttock-squeezers
    Who guide their fingers up their interns' blouses,
And, leaning closer, give themselves permission
To press on them the size of their ambition.

XIII

In Hollywood, each day a smart white guy—
    A self-defined tastemaker and cool dude,
Who knows when to zip or upzip his fly,
    Is learning that he also can be screwed
Without a chance to ask the question *Why?*
    His *nolle prosequi*, preening attitude,
Has been seen through: he's not a streaking comet,
Just someone who makes each who meets him vomit.

XIV

I wish I understood the mad belief
    That it would be sage (either as a prank)
And just good-natured fun (or a relief)
    To take your plonker out and blithely wank
In front of other folks. Is such a brief
    And sordid, desultory thrill—to spank

In Hollywood. Beginning in November, with the revelations concerning sexual abuse, assault, and predation by Hollywood producer Harvey Weinstein, a parade of male notables in entertainment, politics, and elsewhere were accused of sexual misconduct and forced to resign their positions. Also referenced here is comedian Louis C.K.
Nolle prosequi. Latin: literally "be unwilling to follow (or to prosecute)".
Plonker. British slang for penis.

The monkey and hasten your ruination—
Worth seven seconds of ejaculation?

XV

Like most men I possess an average willy,
    It does what it's required to do (per norm).
But waving it about in public's silly—
    Do these men really envisage a swarm
Of people competing to pop their chili
    Into their mouths and gobble up the warm
And fragrant juices? It could be stupidity,
But this ain't courtship, it's insane cupidity.

XVI

Who thinks a fourteen-year-old is fair game
    No matter whether they're a girl or boy?
When I was that age, I could barely frame
    What gay or straight meant, what desire or joy
My body might respond to, or what name
    It could be given. Therefore to destroy
A fragile sense of self, use as a tool,
And exercise one's power, seems too cruel.

XVII

These men seem to assume that every room
    Awaits with bated breath their entry to it;
That without them the flowers will not bloom;
    No plan is worthy for they have seen through it;
That everything's around them to consume,
    And nothing valuable unless they do it.

Fourteen-year-old. Judge Roy Moore, the G.O.P. candidate for the U.S. Senate from Alabama, was accused by several women that he'd behaved inappropriately with them when they were girls. Actor Kevin Spacey was accused of inappropriate sexual behavior with a boy who was a minor.

No one can quench the vastness of their greed
Or fathom the presumptions of their need.

XVIII

I've also felt the urgency of lust,
 How it can shut out logic and self-checks.
But I'm not one who wonders when his bust
 Will sit within the Pantheon; or expects
Women to faint with glee (or burst with lust)
 At just the thought of engaging in sex
With me; or thinks a woman's secret garden
Moistens at the mere notion I've a hard-on.

XIX

È vero, it's an exercise in power,
 A chance to show who's tops, who's grabbed the rings
(And breasts and crotches): the man of the hour.
 The genius who's walked with tsars and kings,
His insights fall like petals in a bower
 Upon his grateful acolytes: what things
He promises! What wit, what style, what grace!
Who cares he told you to sit on his face?

XX

Now, I received the sort of education
 That led me to conclude that when I spoke
A reverent hush would fall upon the nation
 And what I said would (usually at a stroke)
Calm souls and crises. The ensuing ovation
 (Long and inherently deserved) would stoke
The embers of the coldest hearts. And me?
I'd smile and nod with polished modesty.

È Vero. Italian for "Of course."

XXI

So in the panicked, half-assed, bland confessions
  It's easy for me to see calculation:
Of how the consequences of transgressions
  Might be considered; how a declaration
Of sorrow and regret and promised sessions
  Of treatment might soften an allegation;
With the result, after an apt duration,
Tearful, remorseful rehabilitation.

XXII

No shit! The bully-in-chief, Big Kahuna,
  The biggest pussy-grabber of them all
Sits in the Oval Office (*O Fortuna!*):
  Letting his vulgar, clammy fingers crawl
Into the Constitution's each lacuna.
  Probing for weakness, grubby hands now maul
Each tuck and fold of Liberty's green shroud
To prove how generously he's endowed.

XXIII

And yet it matters not—not yet at least—
  To those who voted for him. They've now moved
Beyond his empty promises; have ceased
  To hope their lives will ever be improved
By anyone. Instead, each day they feast
  Upon his diatribes; the primal, grooved,
Well-trodden lines of grievance and indictment:
One half is entertainment, half excitement.

O Fortuna! Fortuna is the Roman goddess of Fortune.
Lacuna. A hole, commonly in an argument or text.

XXIV

Because of that, I wonder if he'll bore them;
    They'll tire of the claptrap, turn the channel
To other pastimes that they see before them.
    In desperation, will he duck and flannel,
Cajole or flatter, whine, moan, or implore them,
    Calling them out as losers as they impanel
A jury to impeach him for his crimes:
The very best and very worst of times?

XXV

Bob Mueller has moved in on Manafort,
    The dodgy, self-enriching, wheeler-dealer.
We sense they've got a strong case, of the sort
    That turns a wiseacre into a squealer,
Especially if he's induced to short
    More serious charges by sending a feeler
Or two out that might meet Bob Mueller's wishes,
By pointing him to much, much larger fishes.

XXVI

They got a guilty plea from Papadopoulos
    Some weeks ago. It's likely that he's worn
A wire for rendezvous in the metropolis,
    In hotel suites and back rooms, and has sworn
To spill. Not since Pericles on the Acropolis
    Poured forth upon Cimon his righteous scorn,
Have citizens felt dispositions hearten:
Perhaps Mueller will ostracize this Spartan!

Flannel. British slang for speaking plausible nonsense.

XXVII

Talking of which, he's found a new occasion
    To talk up Russia, Putin, and defame
Americans in government. The evasion
    About his business dealings, and his blame
For fake news on the media make persuasion
    Much easier that there's a hidden shame
Within the Russian story. And I feel
We've not heard the last of Christopher Steele.

XXVIII

The Steele dossier is the Brit spy's report
    That colored De Sade's views in Canto IV;
Of girls, stained sheets, and squalid deals, the sort
    Of stories that were laughed at as folklore,
Just oppo propaganda. Manafort
    And other witnesses may underscore
How much of Steele's drip-drip-drip revelation
Checks out, and where next heads the investigation.

XXIX

Steele may lay bare another stupid fecker
    Who let John Thomas piss away his brain;
Who had to prove he had the longest pecker,
    And thus poured his career down the drain.
Along the way, he'll do his best to wreck a
    Home, child, administration, and campaign,
Because he had to show that, though a prick,
He was, and will remain, the biggest dick.

Fecker. Irish euphemism. Substitute the first "e" with a "u."
John Thomas. English slang for the penis.

XXX

The danger is that he'll collapse the state
    Before they get him to resign: call out
His base to march on D.C.; throw his weight
    Behind Steve Bannon's talk of coups, and flout
Each law and custom; publicly berate
    Those who "destroyed" him; and (in sum) cast doubt
On our institutions. In this way,
Vladimir Vladimirovich will hold sway.

Canto XII

December 2017

I

Wounded and dazed, we've made it through the year.
    We're still alive, though threatened every day
By tweets and tantrums. A low-level fear
    Thrums in each resident. Meanwhile, away
From sight, the undocumented disappear
    And covenants fall into disarray:
Each news chyron displays a media pasha
Uncovered as a groper or a flasher.

II

Have we learned anything we didn't know
    In January? Have we changed at all?
Are the divisions of a year ago
    Merely more visible, or does a fall—
A single, shocking, overwhelming blow—
    Await? Will finally the toxic pall
Suspended over us evaporate,
Or will a nuclear blast annihilate

Chyron. The news crawl at the bottom of the screen on cable television.

III

Korea and us? Will honesty and facts
 Have any purchase? Will the mandarins
And pundits on the right who made their pacts
 With this unstable boor repent their sins,
And recognize that sometimes one man's acts
 Are so repellent that they outdo "wins"
At any cost? And should we fear that beckoning
For all of us will be a day of reckoning?

IV

Perhaps. Perhaps the endless *Sturm und Drang*
 We live within is really but the quiet
Before the psychic ground cracks with a bang
 Or slowly sinks beneath us. Though a riot
And protests may break out, the well-heeled gang
 Who planned the heist won't cop it. They'll deny it
Was anything to do with them, and state
That all they've tried to do is make us "great."

V

Mike Flynn has pleaded guilty—he who claimed
 If he'd done one-tenth of what *she'd* committed
(Referring to she who could not be named
 Without an epithet), he'd be outfitted
With ankle braces. Well, we can't be blamed
 For hoping counterfeiters are outwitted
For once; and more—that Flynn will tell the G-man
What's needed to ensure that he's a free man.

Sturm und Drang. German for "storm and stress."
If he'd done. Flynn made this argument at the Republican National Convention in July
 2016.

VI

It's mooted that young Jared will be next:
  He of the dimpled cheeks and vacant stare.
It's hard to imagine that he isn't hexed
  Simply by being so close to the lair
Where growls the wounded, maned one. What pretext
  Will *he* devise so that each son and heir
Is punished for their deeds on his behalf,
And he can lay the fault on zealous staff?

VII

It's striking how this young administration
  Has cycled through so many of its own.
Disgraced, resigned, let go—each abjuration
  Predictably ends with them being thrown
Out on their ears. A small consolation
  For former staffers is they're not alone:
A veritable army of the banned,
Could march on D.C. and raise their right hand.

VIII

If Jared's sunk, what will Ivanka do?
  Will she accept her husband's going to jail
To save her daddy's skin, or look into
  A plea so that the family brand won't fail
If father is impeached? Will she smile through
  It all as she hammers a well-pared nail
Into her pater's coffin? Then, as boss,
Will she make more gold of the empire's dross?

IX

You sense beneath the placid insipidity
    A mind that's busy making calculations;
Appraising pros and cons with some fluidity,
    Surfing the tidal waves of allegations
With poised and carefully disguised avidity.
    No doubt her measurement of fluctuations
In Dad's appeal will reap their rewards:
He'll sit in prison, while she sits on boards.

X

And if not she, perhaps Melania Knauss?
    What sweet payback is bubbling in her head
For all the jibes she's suffered from her spouse?
    What murmured, half-confessions in their bed
Might she disclose? What compromising grouse,
    Suggestive clue, or insight might she shed?
If she could safeguard her share and her son
Then what tidbits she'll spill before she's done!

XI

Is she concocting plans behind those shades?
    Are her glossed lips sealed by more than Botox?
Does she squint at him as his aura fades
    Because she's grasped how soon her fly-blown fox
Will feel the hens' revenge? The sad charades
    Of standing by your men although their cocks
And fingers wander . . . what might be her plan
To, in one gesture, stick it to The Man?

XII

Is it fantastical to think each lady
    Will move in concert when the time is right
And grab him right back? Could he be afraid he
    Has lit the fuse that one day will ignite
A blaze that can't be doused, and every shady,
    Illegal exploit will be brought to light;
That even those who've studiously ignored
The nightmares will say, "Throw him overboard"?

XIII

The strategy so far has been to pour
    Contempt upon the accusers, and berate
Those who'd even *consider* that Roy Moore,
    For instance, is not someone whom the state
Of Alabama should cast their vote for,
    Or a man whom you'd like your kid to date.
Why let a little thing like child predation
Stand in the way of Judge Moore's elevation?

XIV

The times call for more female leadership
    Given how many men have feet of clay.
A few slimebags and supercreeps may trip,
    Yet they've not fallen yet. Meanwhile, their prey,
Exposed to trolls and bots are left with zip
    But pleas for something like closure one day.
"Refute, dispute, impute, mute" show hardliners
You can survive assault charges on minors.

To trolls and bots. Trolls are individuals who post offensive or insulting comments on sites in order to generate controversy and traffic to the site. Bots are machines programmed to do the same.

XV

How touchingly naive we are to think
    That such reports would make the G.O.P.
Reject or force a candidate to blink
    And step aside! Since Clinton (*he* not she)
Did much the same and charges didn't sink
    His re-election or presidency,
Then why not parse, deny, and wait it out?
The playbook worked: when in doubt, then cast doubt.

XVI

Meanwhile, the lives of silent desperation
    Continue: raddled, riddled bodies found
Collapsed in the men's toilet at the station
    Or near the fields the kids play on; or drowned
In one of the small creeks; a sad oblation
    To consecrate the unforgiving ground
With poppy-blood, which stains its vivid red
Like scarlet letters on the living dead.

XVII

You see their sleepless nodding on the street,
    Bent double, swaying gently in the breeze,
As if they are examining their feet
    Or strange plantations of exotic trees;
Curled up on benches, or seeking the heat
    Of subway vents so that they do not freeze:
Contracted pupils, bodies limp and slack,
The telltale signs of the half-death of smack.

Oblation. A sacred offering.
Smack. Slang for heroin.

XVIII

This is one thing that all of us now share:
    Communities across the U.S.A.,
Flooded by this expression of despair,
    Call for assistance, someone who will say
Their pain is heard and not another prayer;
    Who marshals resources that will convey
To areas of blight good jobs and hope
That's truly federal in cash and scope.

XIX

Another thing we share is our rage.
    Facts, policy, and history are infested
By false equivalence. Each Facebook page
    Is splattered with fake news: myths we've invested
With totems and taboos we use to gauge
    How furious we should be—until they're bested
By even more frenzied denunciations,
Colored by arbitrary execrations.

XX

And I'm as guilty as the rest of them:
    My arms carving the air, head in my hands.
With rolling eyes, I bellow (specks of phlegm
    Upon my lips) that no one understands
How wretched things are, how we must condemn
    All those who voted for him. My demands
For "something to be done" aren't acted on.
Conspiracy! Betrayal! All chance gone!

XXI

These fever fits, however, bring no closer
    A resolution that delivers healing.
For every downer—something even grosser
    That has me gasping and all senses reeling—
Another person gets a rush-filled dose, a
    Much-wished-for righteous lift, without a ceiling.
For hits of joy or rage, who would avoid a
Mainlining of such endless *Schadenfreude*?

XXII

And that, it's true, is what he's hoping for,
    On which his presidency's predicated.
That it is *him* we worship or abhor
    Is all that matters: we must not be sated,
Indifferent, or dulled; we must want more.
    Whether we are dejected or elated,
He'll act without restraint so he can train us
To focus on him, let him entertain us.

XXIII

In his convention speech, he made the claim
    That he alone could fix what had gone wrong
With the U.S. Just mentioning his name
    Would make forgotten men burst into song.
No longer would we feel a sense of shame
    At being left behind, or (in vain) long
For a lost past. He would reverse the date
And bring us to the prelapsarian state.

Schadenfreude. German for joy in someone else's suffering.

XXIV

Most of that rambling speech was plainly crap.
    One thing was true: he was, and is, the fix.
We're all hooked on him now: each day we wrap
    The tourniquet of news around us; pricks
Inject plague-ridden cocktails of foul pap
    Into the sickened body's politics.
We spend the days and nights strung out and wired;
Loathing ourselves for what we've most desired.

XXV

Unable to think outside the addiction
    We cannot see the way the crooks and thieves
Are stealing what we own, selling the fiction
    That, since at some time everyone deceives,
Nothing is not for sale, and that conviction
    And continence are dumb. He who believes
The weak will be rewarded, strong brought low,
Is a failed, lyin' loser and a schmo.

XXVI

In this way, he has made us in his image.
    Petulant, easy to offend, and tribal,
We turn debates into a form of scrimmage
    Where questioners are pounced upon, and libel
Is summoned up on those with but a slim, midge-
    Sized disagreement. Or we throw a Bible
At anyone who doubts, so we can scuttle
What's thoughtful, measured, reasonable, and subtle.

XXVII

No one is guilty, no one innocent.
　　The high road's potholed and the moral heights
Have been bulldozed and razed. Meanwhile, cement
　　Has been poured on the common ground; the nights
That once beheld a bright dawn are now spent
　　In fitful, sleepless tossing. While the lights
Of faith that once illumined us are dying,
Extinguished by the endless, endless lying.

XXVIII

He's made us all as crazy and untethered
　　As he is. Madcap days pass in a flurry
Of tweets, alerts, and blogs that must be weathered
　　And not reflected on; a kind of slurry
Seeps into our mind's groundwater, blethered
　　And toxic filings that scar and burn, worry
The conscience, spirits blanch, leave souls abraded:
A dump where freedom's soil is degraded.

XXIX

Coarsened, obsessive, guzzling down the junk,
　　We splutter to the ending of December,
Aware that, though it may indeed be bunk,
　　We'll beg that next year's one we will remember
Not as the nightmare that was this one. Drunk,
　　We'll toast the future, as the final ember
Of these twelve sad months at last fades away
Leaving us bitter ashes, cold and gray.

Blethered. Long-winded.
Abraded. Worn thin or ragged by erosion or overuse.

XXX

But it's from ashes that the phoenix rises:
  More women now run for a seat in power.
If nothing else, we can expect surprises
  If not each minute, surely by the hour.
If Bob Mueller is fired, or arises
  A crisis where the usual pout and glower
Is not enough to hold forces at bay,
Then the old hound dog will have his last day.

XXXI

By this time next year it could all be done:
  His office, future of a free world, life!
He could be lying in jail or the sun;
  He could be shacked up with a brand-new wife
In Florida, pardoned by Pence. More fun,
  A new House could be sharpening the knife
To slash at backroom deals, graft, and sleaze.
To which I say, "Oh God. If Only. Please."

Dramatis Personae

Adams, John (1735–1826). Second President of the United States (1797–1801). Two of Adams' sons, Charles and Thomas, became alcoholics and failed in the legal profession.

Ailes, Roger (1940–2017). Conservative chairman and CEO of Fox News, who resigned in July 2016 after being accused of sexual misconduct, and died in May 2017.

Al-Assad, Bashar (b. 1965). President of Syria. Since 2011, his government has killed hundreds of thousands of its own citizens, including using chemical weapons against them.

Alt-right. Name claimed by the resurgent far-right, white-nationalist movement, which contains many features of the KKK, including anti-Semitism, racism, and neo-Nazism.

Antifa. Antifascist activists and protesters, whom right-wing critics claim foment violence against law-abiding citizens supporting a white-supremacist agenda.

Baldwin, James (1924–1987). Novelist and social critic, and subject of the 2017 documentary film *I Am Not Your Negro* by Raoul Peck.

Bannon, Steve (b. 1953). Media and political activist who ran the G.O.P. presidential nominee's campaign after the resignation of Paul Manafort (q.v.) in July 2016 and entered the administration as White House chief strategist. Bannon left in August 2017 to return to the extreme right-wing website Breitbart News, from which he was forced to resign in January 2018.

Beyoncé (b. 1981). R&B megastar who sang at the 2009 Inauguration gala of Barack (q.v.) and Michelle Obama (q.v.). Her full name is Beyoncé Knowles. She is married to Jay Z (q.v.).

Buchanan, James (1791–1868). Fifteenth President of the United States (1857–1861).

Burns, Ken (b. 1953). Documentary filmmaker, whose ten-episode series *The Vietnam War* (coproduced with Lynn Novick) ran on PBS in Fall 2017.

Bush, Billy (b. 1971). TV host. In 2005, Bush was a reporter on the NBC TV show *Access Hollywood* in which, in an off-camera moment, the 2016 G.O.P. presidential nominee (in his previous incarnation as the then-star of the TV show *The Apprentice*) was taped boasting of assaulting women. Bush's servile giggling led to him being fired in 2017 from his job on the *Today* show.

Bush, George W. (b. 1946). Forty-third President of the United States (2001–2009). During the first few months of his presidency, Bush took many golfing vacations.

Bush, John Ellis (Jeb) (b. 1953). Ex-governor of Florida who ran for nomination in the 2016 G.O.P. presidential primaries. Brother of President George W. Bush (q.v.).

Bush, Neil (b. 1955). Brother of George (q.v.) and Jeb Bush (q.v.), whose role in the Savings & Loan financial scandal of the 1980s caused some embarrassment for his father, President George H. W. Bush, the forty-first President of the United States.

Byron, Lord (1788–1824). Born George Gordon, the poet became Sixth Baron Byron of Rochdale when he was ten years old.

Carter, Billy (1937–1988). Brother of President Jimmy Carter, the thirty-ninth President of the United States, whose business dealings with Libya and other more personal failings embarrassed the Carter presidency.

Ceauşescu, Nicolae (1918–1989). Dictator of Romania, who was toppled from power and shot, following the collapse of the Berlin Wall.

Chaffetz, Jason (b. 1967). The Utah Republican was Chair of the House Oversight Committee before resigning from the chairmanship and the House of Representatives in June 2017.

Cimon (510–450 BCE). Athenian statesman who supported the Spartans during the helot uprising and was ostracized by Pericles (q.v.).

Clinton, Hillary (b. 1947). Former First Lady, U.S. Secretary of State during the first Obama administration, and the Democratic Party's nominee for president in 2016. Her husband, Bill, the forty-second President of the United States (1993–2001), was involved in a number of sex scandals both before and during his administration, many of which were weaponized by the Republican nominee during the 2016 presidential campaign.

Clinton, Roger (b. 1956). Half-brother of President Bill Clinton (see above), whose financial and drug troubles embarrassed the Clinton White House.

Collins, Susan (b. 1952). Republican. Senior Senator from Maine.

Corker, Bob (b. 1952). Republican. Junior Senator from Tennessee. Corker, a vocal critic of the President, announced he'd retire from the Senate in 2018.

Cornyn, John (b. 1952). Republican. Senior Senator from Texas.

Cruz, Ted (b. 1970). Republican. Junior Senator from Texas, and candidate for the 2016 G.O.P. nomination for president. The eventual G.O.P. nominee nicknamed him "Lyin' Ted."

De Sade, Marquis (1740–1814). Satirist and pornographer, whose most famous work is *120 Days of Sodom.*

Darrow, Clarence (1857–1938). Lawyer who famously defended John Scopes, who was indicted for teaching the theory of evolution in Tennessee.

Dennett, Daniel (b. 1942). American writer, philosopher of the mind, and cognitive scientist.

Dowd, Maureen (b. 1952). Social satirist of New York and Washington's social scene, and liberal columnist for *The New York Times.*

Du Bois, W. E. B. (1868–1963). Writer of *The Souls of Black Folk* (1903) and co-founder of the National Association for the Advancement of Colored People (NAACP).

Duterte, Rody (b. 1945). President of the Philippines. Duterte has openly admitted to extrajudicial killings in a war against drugs in his country, in which more than 7,000 people have been killed.

Erdoğan, Recep Tayyip (b. 1954). Turkish President. A failed coup against him in 2016 led to the further consolidation of his power and repression of dissent in 2017.

Flake, Jeff (b. 1962). Republican. Junior Senator from Arizona. In a speech in the Senate in October 2017, Flake announced he would not seek re-election in 2018 and criticized the current incumbent in the White House.

Flynn, Mike (b. 1958). Retired Lt. General, chosen by the 2016 President-Elect as his National Security Advisor. Flynn was forced to resign in February 2017 for lying to Congress about meetings with Russian officials in December 2016. He pleaded guilty to lying to the F.B.I. in December 2017.

Friedan, Betty (1921–2006). Author of *The Feminine Mystique* (1963), one of the foundational texts of "second-wave" feminism.

Gingrich, Newt (b. 1943). Republican. Former Speaker of the House of Representatives, Fox News pundit, presidential candidate, and supporter of 45.

Giuliani, Rudolf (b. 1944). Republican. Two-time mayor of New York City, candidate for president, and supporter of 45.

Glenn, John (1921–2016). Air force officer and first astronaut to orbit the Earth. He became a Democratic U.S. senator from Colorado.

Gorka, Sebastian (b. 1970). Controversial British-born political and strategic advisor to the President, who resigned in August 2017.

Graham, Lindsey (b. 1955). Republican. Senior Senator from South Carolina, 2016 G.O.P. presidential candidate.

Hanh, Thich Nhat (b. 1926). Vietnamese Buddhist monk known for his work on nonviolence and meditation, and the author of several books, including *Peace Is Every Step* and *The Miracle of Mindfulness*.

Harding, Warren (1865–1923). Twenty-ninth President of the United States (1921–1923).

Heller, Joseph (1923–1999). Satirist and the writer of *Catch-22* (1962), which features the character of Major Major (q.v.).

Heyer, Heather (d. 2017). Social justice activist who was deliberately run over and killed during a white-supremacist rally in Charlottesville, Virginia, in August 2017.

Homer. Greek author of the *Iliad* and *Odyssey*.

Jackson, Andrew (1767–1845). Seventh President of the United States (1829–1837), responsible for the forced relocations and many deaths of Native Americans.

Jay Z (b. 1969). Popular rapper and producer (a.k.a. Shawn Carter), and frequent visitor (with his wife Beyoncé Knowles [q.v.]) to the White House during the Obama (q.v.) administration.

Jefferson, Thomas (1743–1826). Third President of the United States (1801–1809). Considered one of the Founding Fathers of the Republic.

Julio-Claudians. Dynastic family that produced all Roman emperors from Augustus (d. 14) to Nero (q.v.).

Kennedy, John F. (1917–1963). Thirty-fifth President of the United States (1961–1963), who narrowly avoided World War III in the confrontation with the U.S.S.R. during the Cuban Missile Crisis in 1962.

Kim Jong-un (b. 1984?). Leader of North Korea (D.P.R.K.). During 2016 and 2017, Kim conducted several nuclear tests, including firing missiles over the Sea of Japan. Kim also indulged in name-calling with the U.S. President.

Khrushchev, Nikita (1894–1971). Soviet premier after Stalin, who confronted the U.S. in the Cuban Missile Crisis.

Ku Klux Klan. White-supremacist, anti-Semitic terrorist group, responsible for murders, lynchings, and arson in the U.S. from the end of the Civil War onward.

Kushner, Jared (b. 1981). Media and real estate tycoon and 45's son-in-law. Kushner was given a large portfolio in the administration.

Lin, Maya (b. 1957). Architect, most famously of the Vietnam Veterans Memorial in Washington, D.C.

Manafort, Paul (b. 1949). Campaign manager for the G.O.P. nominee for president from June to August 2016. Prior to this, Manafort worked for Viktor Yanukovych, before the latter was ousted as president of Ukraine in February 2014.

McCain, John (b. 1936). Republican. Senior Senator from Arizona, and G.O.P. presidential nominee in 2008. McCain was diagnosed with brain cancer in July 2017, and was the casting vote against the repeal of Obamacare in the Senate in September 2017.

McCarthy, Joseph (1908–1957). Republican. Senator from Wisconsin, who led a series of investigations/"witch hunts" into supposed Communist infiltration of various U.S. institutions in 1954. His name is a byword for politicized character assassination.

McConnell, Mitch (b. 1942). Republican. Senior Senator from Kentucky and Senate Majority Leader.

Medicis. Family of politicians, bankers, popes, and patrons of the arts in Florence during the Renaissance.

Mix, Tom (1880–1940). Hollywood actor, who appeared in numerous Westerns between 1909 and 1935.

Moore, Roy (b. 1947). Conservative judge and Republican candidate for the senate from Alabama, who lost to Democrat Doug Jones in a special election on December 12, 2017. Several women accused Moore of inappropriate sexual contact when they were teenagers and, in one case, a minor.

Mueller, Robert (b. 1944). Republican. Former Director of the F.B.I. In May 2017, after the President fired F.B.I. director James Comey in February, and Attorney General Jeff Sessions (q.v.) recused himself, Deputy Attorney General Rod Rosenstein (q.v.) appointed Mueller to be special counsel for the Department of Justice in an investigation of links between Russia and the G.O.P. campaign during the 2016 presidential election campaign.

Murkowski, Lisa (b. 1957). Republican. Senior Senator from Alaska.

Mussolini, Benito (1883–1945). Fascist dictator of Italy, 1925–1945, known for striking poses.

Nero (37–68). Tyrannical emperor of Rome, who played music while Rome burned.

Nixon, Richard (b. 1913–1994). Thirty-sixth President of the United States (1969–1974), who resigned in disgrace rather than be impeached. Known as "Tricky Dick."

Obama, Barack (b. 1961). Forty-fourth President of the United States (2009–2017). His father, a Kenyan, whose own father had converted to Islam, met his mother, in Hawaii, where the president was born.

Obama, Michelle (b. 1964). Very popular First Lady and wife of Barack Obama (q.v.).

O'Reilly, Bill (b. 1949). Long-time Fox News host and pugnacious conservative. Fired in April 2017 after several women complained of sexual misconduct. It was discovered that O'Reilly had settled several lawsuits on the same issue.

Page, Carter (b. 1971). Advisor to the G.O.P. presidential nominee, whose ties and visits to Russia during the 2016 campaign came under scrutiny in January 2017.

Papadopoulos, George (b. 1987). Advisor to the G.O.P. presidential nominee who in October 2016 pleaded guilty to misleading F.B.I. investigators as part of the Mueller (q.v.) investigation.

Pence, Mike (b. 1959) Republican. Forty-eighth Vice-President of the United States (2017–).

Pericles (494–429 BCE). Famous orator and leader of Athens. He ostracized Cimon (q.v.).

Price, Tom (b. 1954). Former Republican congressman who became Secretary of Health and Human Services in January 2017. Having failed to get Obamacare-repeal passed and accused of using public money on expensive travel, Price resigned from office in September 2017.

Priebus, Reince (b. 1972). Former head of the Republican National Committee who became 45's Chief of Staff in January 2017. He resigned in July 2017.

Putin, Vladimir Vladimirovich (b. 1952). President of Russia. The nature and extent of Russia's meddling in the 2016 election was a constant conversation throughout 2017—as was the nature and extent of the collusion of the Republican presidential candidate's campaign and the candidate's own knowledge of such collusion, and potentially compromised status.

Rabelais, François (1483–1553). Satirist whose work and characters are often grotesque and obscene, such as in *Gargantua and Pantagruel*.

Roof, Dylann (b. 1994). White-supremacist murderer of nine parishioners of the Emanuel African Methodist Episcopal Church in Charleston, South Carolina on June 17, 2015.

Rosenstein, Rod (b. 1965). Deputy Attorney General of the United States.

Ryan, Paul (b. 1970). Republican. Speaker of the House of Representatives.

Sanders, Bernie (b. 1941). Independent. Junior Senator from Vermont, and socialist, who was the main rival of Hillary Clinton (q.v.) to be the Democratic Party's nominee for president in 2016.

Sanders, Sarah Huckabee (b. 1982). White House Press Secretary from July 2017, after the resignation of Sean Spicer (q.v.).

Sasse, Ben (b. 1972). Republican. Junior Senator from Nebraska.

Scaramucci, Anthony (b. 1964). White House Communications Director, who lasted only eleven days on the job before resigning after an obscenity-laden phone call with a reporter. Also known as "The Mooch."

Schumer, Chuck (b. 1950). Democrat. Senior Senator from New York, and the Senate Minority Leader.

Scorsese, Martin (b. 1942). Film director known for his elaborately staged scenes of violence.

Spicer, Sean (b. 1971). First White House Press Secretary in the current administration, he was widely pilloried for his performance. He resigned in July 2017.

Steele, Christopher (b. 1964). British spy whose dossier on the G.O.P. presidential nominee's links with Russian real estate and politically connected individuals, especially around the 2013 Miss World pageant in Moscow, was endowed with varying degrees of credibility in 2016 and 2017.

Stone, Roger (b. 1952). Political "dirty tricks" operative and long-time supporter of the current White House resident.

Swift, Jonathan (1667–1745). Irish satirist, known for his scatological humor. Writer of *Gulliver's Travels*.

Tasso, Torquato (1544–1595). With other Italian poets, such as Boccaccio and Ariosto, he wrote epic verse in *ottava rima*, which in the English form consists of iambic pentameters in an *ababbcc* rhyme pattern. Classical poets were expected to have served poetic apprenticeships writing shorter verse forms (such as sonnets, odes, or epigrams), before trying ambitious epics.

Thiong'o, Ngugi wa (b. 1938). Kenyan political and social satirist, known for his long novel *Wizard of the Crow*.

Thune, John (b. 1961). Republican. Senior Senator from South Dakota.

Tillerson, Rex (b. 1952). Former CEO of Exxon Mobil who was appointed Secretary of State by 45.

Toomey, Pat (b. 1961). Republican. Senior Senator from Pennsylvania.

Trump, Jr., Donald J. (b. 1977). The oldest son of 45 and enthusiastic big-game hunter.

Trump, Eric (b. 1984). Middle son of 45.

Trump, Ivanka (b. 1981). Daughter of 45, married to Jared Kushner (q.v.). Both she and her husband were widely, if erroneously, expected to exert a moderating influence on the President.

Trump, Melania (née Knauss) (b. 1970). First Lady of the United States, 45's third wife, and mother of his youngest son. During and after the Inauguration, Melania understandably often appeared crestfallen, furious, frosty, irritated, and disconsolate when her husband addressed her, or was in his company.

Van Buren, Martin (1782–1862). Eighth President of the United States (1837–1841).

Virgil (70–19 BCE). Roman poet. Author of the *Aeneid*, and Dante's guide in the *Inferno* and *Purgatorio* of his *Divina Commedia*.

Waltz, Christoph (b. 1956). Austro-German actor who played a Nazi officer in Quentin Tarantino's 2009 movie *Inglourious Basterds*.

Washington, George (1732–1799). First President of the United States (1789–1797).

Weiner, Anthony (b. 1964). Former Democratic congressman from New York, who pleaded guilty to "sexting" a minor in May 2017 and was sentenced to prison in September.

Wilson, Woodrow (1856–1924). Twenty-eighth President of the United States (1913–1921).

Xi Jinping (b. 1953). General Secretary of the Communist Party and President of China since 2013.

Greco-Roman Mythological Characters and Places

Aeneas. Legendary Trojan, whose travels and eventual arrival in Italy form the *Aeneid* by Augustan poet Virgil (q.v.).

Amazon. Member of a race of fearless warrior women.

Apollo. God of the arts.

Calliope. Muse of epic poetry.

Charon. Ferryman who carried the dead, after they had paid a coin for passage, over the River Styx (q.v.) in Hades (q.v.).

Hades. Region known as the Underworld, where the dead live.

Hermes. God of communication, commerce, trickery, theft, and guide to the Underworld. Known to the Romans as Mercury (q.v.).

Mercury (see Hermes).

Midas. King of Crete, notorious for his insatiable love of gold.

Nyx. Goddess of night.

Odysseus. King of Ithaca, whose return from the Trojan War is depicted in the *Odyssey*.

Orpheus. Musician and poet who visits the Underworld, guided by Hermes (q.v.), to rescue his love Eurydice from the dead.

Parnassus. Mountain home of Apollo and the Muses.

Penelope. Wife of Odysseus (q.v.), who faithfully waits for his return after twenty years of being away.

Pygmalion. Sculptor and worshiper of Venus, who fell in love with his own creation.

Silenus. Drunken and pleasure-seeking satyr and companion of Dionysos, the god of wine.

Styx. River of the Underworld.

Sybil. Prophetess at the shrine of Apollo (q.v.) in Cumae, who is Aeneas' (q.v.) guide to the Underworld.

Tartarus. A prison within Hades.

Telemachus. Son of Odysseus. In the *Odyssey*, Telemachus and his father get rid of the marriage suitors to Penelope.

Ulysses (see Odysseus).

Other Literary Characters

Alexander, Susan. Indifferent opera-singer and second wife of publishing magnate Charles Foster Kane in Orson Welles' *Citizen Kane*.

Amber. One of the DNAgents in the series published by Eclipse Comics.

Bluebeard. Terrifying, mysterious property owner in folklore. My reference is Béla Bartók's opera *Bluebeard's Castle* (1918).

Braggadocio. Empty, boastful, and vain braggart in Edmund Spenser's *The Faerie Queene* (1590).

Britomart. Righteous warrior and heroine of Edmund Spenser's *The Faerie Queene*.

Bueller, Ferris. Eponymous hero of John Hughes' 1986 movie, *Ferris Bueller's Day Off*, who has little interest in school.

Catwoman. Superhero crime fighter of DC Comics.

Corleone, Don. Mob boss in *The Godfather*, Mario Puzo's novel about the Mafia.

DuBois, Blanche. Melodramatic character in *A Streetcar Named Desire*, a 1947 play by Tennessee Williams.

Dug. Talking dog in the Pixar animation studios 2009 movie *Up!*

Falstaff, Sir John. Vain, cowardly, fat, witty, and drunken knight in William Shakespeare's *Henry IV* parts 1 and 2, and *The Merry Wives of Windsor*.

Finch, Atticus. Lawyer and hero against racism of Harper Lee's 1960 novel *To Kill a Mockingbird*.

Gimli. Dwarf in J. R. R. Tolkien's trilogy *The Lord of the Rings*. His battle-axe's name (translated into English) is "throng-cleaver."

Kane, Charles Foster. Eponymous anti-hero of Orson Welles' *Citizen Kane* (1941). The film depicts the older Kane controlling and attempting to mold his wife, Susan Alexander (q.v.), to his own wishes.

Krueger, Freddy. Main character in the sequence of horror films that began with 1984's *A Nightmare on Elm Street*, directed by Wes Craven. Krueger's signature weapon was his gloves with claws extending from the fingers.

Kylo Ren. Male character in the film *The Force Awakens* (2015), part of the *Star Wars* franchise.

Lady Liberty. Personification of a statue in New York City harbor.

Major Major. Nonentity in *Catch-22*, a 1962 comic-satirical novel about World War II by Joseph Heller (q.v.).

Peter Pan. Boy who never grows up in J. M. Barrie's play of the same name.

Sauron. Malevolent magus and eponymous villain of J. R. R. Tolkien's trilogy *The Lord of the Rings*. Sauron in the trilogy is depicted as a disembodied, lidless, and all-seeing eye.

Skimpole, Harold. The disarming sponger depicted in Charles Dickens' 1853 novel *Bleak House*.

Storm. Female X-men superheroine from Marvel Comics.

Titania. Queen of the fairies. In William Shakespeare's *A Midsummer Night's Dream*, she falls in love with Bottom, a commoner, whose head has been turned into that of a donkey's.

Uncle Sam. The personification of the U.S. He is typically portrayed as a tall, thin white man with long white hair and a beard, who wears a stovepipe hat.

X-men. Superheroes and social misfits in Marvel Comics series of the same name.

Wolf Man. Horror movie staple, involving lycanthropy.

Wolverine. A character in Marvel Comics X-men (q.v.) series.

Acknowledgments

The first and greatest thanks must go to my colleague Evander Lomke, whose unflagging enthusiasm for my terrible jokes, wretched accents, and ghastly puns has been a never-ending source of gratified mystification to me. I am deeply appreciative of his willingness to read my monthly effusions and to cast his sober and detailed eyes over the text and to offer his Bronx-born ear to my Britishisms and correct them. Thanks also to Alex Lockwood for offering suggestions on the text at a late stage. I should also like to bow deeply to William Shakespeare for the unparalleled collection of insults that adorn his plays. Over and over again, my bucket and I found ourselves returning to his deep well to draw up a fresh draught of obscenities.

The Trumpiad would not have been possible without the always-reliable companionship of Rhymezone (rhymezone.com), which provided me with invaluable rhymes and synonyms, at any day and night, without judgment as to the adequacy or otherwise of my poor efforts at verse.

About the Author

Martin Rowe is the author of a novel, *Nicaea: A Book of Correspondences* (Lindisfarne, 2003), and three works of non-fiction: *The Polar Bear in the Zoo: A Reflection, The Elephants in the Room: An Excavation* (both Lantern, 2013), and (with Evander Lomke) *Right off the Bat: Baseball, Cricket, Literature, and Life* (Paul Dry, 2011). Martin is also the librettist for *And the Hummingbird Says . . .* , with music by Mihoko Suzuki (2017), and the writer (with sound effects by Tim Cramer) of *Preposterous Pomes and Dotty Ditties: Bonkers Ballards, Loopy Lullabies and Silly Songs for Young and Old* (2013), both of which are available on CD Baby. He lives in Brooklyn, New York. His work can be found at martin-rowe.com, and you can follow him on Facebook at: facebook.com/martinckrowe.

Made in the USA
Middletown, DE
04 April 2018